RISKING IT ALL

RISK SERIES BOOK 3

CAROLINE EASTON

Editing: KL Editing Services.
Cover and Formatting by The Graphics Shed

CONTENTS

Chapter 1	1
Chapter 2	13
Chapter 3	29
Chapter 4	35
Chapter 5	45
Chapter 6	55
Chapter 7	63
Chapter 8	69
Chapter 9	77
Chapter 10	87
Chapter 11	95
Chapter 12	105
Chapter 13	113
Chapter 14	121
Chapter 15	129
Chapter 16	137
Chapter 17	145
Chapter 18	155
Chapter 19	163
Chapter 20	171
Chapter 21	179
Chapter 22	185
Chapter 23	193
Chapter 24	201
Chapter 25	207
Chapter 26	217

Chapter 27   225
Chapter 28   233
Chapter 29   239
Chapter 30   247
Chapter 31   253
Chapter 32   263

Acknowledgments   271
About the Author   273
Other Books   275

CHAPTER One

*S*tepping on stage used to give him the biggest high going; not anymore. That came via the magic white powder that was so freely available to him. Fame had brought Jake Williams a lot of things along the way. One of them being the ability to click his fingers and have his drug of choice hand-delivered to his dressing room door. Now, there he stood in his dressing room with the snow-white powder lined up on the countertop, ready for him. The plastic bag discarded as he tapped his credit card beside the lines of powder, praying inwardly that it would deliver the adrenalin surge he needed to get through the gig.

Lowering his head and covering one nostril, Jake inhaled the powder, waiting for the familiar burn as he sniffed back the dust. Slouching back into the chair, his eyes drifted closed as the feeling of slipping beneath water surrounded his whole body. The pressure pushing against his skin as if he were submerged relaxed each muscle one by one. Each limb felt as though it were floating away from him. All the stress of his everyday life left his body and floated around him, leaving him carefree and happy. A broad grin unfolded across his face.

Jake Williams had it all. Money, fame, but above all, notoriety. The last five years in the music industry had afforded him all the luxuries he could ask for. But that kind of fame didn't come for free. With barely a day off in that time, he'd worked hard and partied harder. To the outside world, his life was enviable. Property, cars, and women all lay in his wake, as did the tabloid headlines and bad press. But who was he to argue? What the fans wanted, the fans got. They demanded bad boy Jake, and they got him. In spades.

"You want me to sort that out for you?" The blonde girl rose from the sofa behind him. Wearing skimpy denim shorts that were barely there, and a T-shirt with some band emblem emblazoned on the front, she looked barely legal. But he relied on his bodyguard to check out that shit for him. He didn't need the hassle of checking their ID. Graham hadn't let him down yet.

The girl moved between his legs and settled on her knees before him. Her hand traced the outline of his erection through his jeans. Yeah, coke did that to him. It was a happy side effect of his recreational usage. The girl's fingers deftly worked at the button fly, granting her access to his cock. Her eyes devoured the length of him as his hard on jutted proudly skyward.

Jake watched her through hooded eyes, and her tongue flicked over her lips as she worked her hand over his silky, hard length.

"Just fucking suck it," he growled impatiently. He didn't need the work up, merely the goods. She was there for a reason and one reason only; to suck him off so he could get on the damn stage. She didn't need asking twice. Wide-eyed, she lowered her mouth to his shaft as she wrapped her lips around him, sliding slowly down his full length, taking as much of him as she could into her mouth.

Her hand gripped his shaft, pumping hard as her mouth worked him over. Jake hissed in pleasure as she engulfed most of his hard cock. Wet, slurping sounds filled the room, heightening his arousal as she sucked greedily at his cock. His hand moved to grip the back of her head as his hips bucked faster, chasing the finishing line. The girl gripped his jeans and pulled them lower, exposing him completely. Her hand cradled his balls as she continued to devour his length. His cock looked magnificent pounding in and out of her mouth as she stared up at him.

Thrusting harder into her mouth, Jake's eyes remained fixed on her lips, watching, as his cock disappeared over and over again, hitting the back of her throat, making her gag as he continued to pound her face. He couldn't even remember her name, but what did that matter? He had no intention of seeing her again.

She hummed around his cock, the vibrations shuddering through him as he chased his release. Increased pressure around his balls caused him to fly over the edge as she swallowed him deep into her throat again.

"Fuuuck!" He gasped, dragging air into his lungs. The girl swallowed audibly before licking around the head of his cock, ensuring he was clean before tucking him back into his boxers.

Rubbing a hand over his face, Jake breathed heavily. He was unsure if it was the coke or the blowjob that had caused his heart to beat insanely fast. Whatever it was, he sure as hell couldn't stand just yet.

"Do you have a pen?" The girl looked around the room as she quizzed him.

"Why?" He tried and failed to stifle a yawn as he spoke.

"I'll write down my number for you, unless you

want me to add it in your phone?" She stood opposite him, her hand held out expectantly.

"No need, sweetheart. I leave town tonight."

"Well, you could call me when you're back in town..."

"I'll have Graham take you to the arena, make sure you're in the best seats. It's been fun." Standing, Jake moved towards the door, opened it, and checked outside for his bodyguard. True to form, Graham sat on a plastic chair, no more than five feet away from Jake's dressing room door.

"Hey, can you show..." He tried desperately to drag her name from the depths of his memory but he couldn't do it. "...this young lady to the arena, please? Thanks, man." Graham chuckled as he stood to escort the girl back to the arena and away from Jake. He noticed the tears in her eyes as she looked longingly up at the star who had already dismissed her and moved on.

"It's Tammy. My name is Tammy," she stated to nobody in particular.

Dragging a tube of mints from his pocket, Graham offered her the packet, squeezing a solitary sweet into her hand as they walked along the industrial corridor towards the arena. "Don't sweat it, sweetheart. Comes with the territory." The lone sniff that echoed down the hallway indicated she was 'sweating it' big time. "Do you know the club in town, The Shed? Me and a few of the other guys will be there tonight after the gig. If you want to join us, I can put your name on the list. But just so we're clear, Jake won't be there. It's only me and a few of the others, chilling out before we pack up the kit tomorrow." They paused before the double doors which would take her to the auditorium. Graham watched her with expectant eyes. He didn't often pick up Jake's seconds, but this one was cute and he felt a little sorry for her. At twenty-nine, he'd spent all his working life in the music industry. He'd seen far too many girls come and go through dressing room doors. Tammy was no different. She wouldn't stand out in the morning, but if he could make her feel even slightly better about herself in the meantime, then why not?

Tammy's eyes lit up with hope. "I'd like that, thanks."

Pushing on the fire door lever, Graham swung the door open for her, indicating the path for her to follow. "Warm up will be on in forty minutes. Enjoy the show. See you later, Tammy."

Heading up the corridor, Graham made his way back to check on Jake. Izzie, Jake's manager, had specifically asked him to not let Jake out of his sight. He'd gone off the rails recently and she was having a hard time keeping tabs on him. Tapping on the door, Graham didn't wait for Jake to allow him entry. Instead, he pushed the steel fire door open and peered inside. His eyes rested on the snoozing star.

Jake lay on the sofa with his jeans still unbuttoned and his hand tucked inside the waistband of his boxers. His bare, tattooed chest heaved as gentle snores escaped him.

"Sweet dreams, Jakey boy." Graham chuckled as he shut the door on the sleeping beauty.

♪ ♪ ♪

The phone vibrated against his leg, stirring him from his haze-like state. The ringtone he'd set for his manager used to evoke all things good in him; now it merely irritated him. Fishing around in his pocket, Jake swiped his thumb across the screen, sending the call to voicemail. He didn't need another lecture. She repeated the same old shit to him day after day. Why she couldn't leave him alone to do his job was beyond him.

His eyes scanned the room. The usual devastation met his glare. Discarded clothes - mostly from groupies

- empty bottles, and food trash littered every surface. The only thing that held his attention were the small clear plastic bags that lay discarded on the counter. Sitting up on the sofa, Jake rested his elbows on his knees, rubbing his hands over his face, trying to erase the groggy feeling that still owned him. The banging on the door startled him, but before he could call out for them to come in, the door pushed open and one of the runners said, "Five minutes to stage, Mr Williams."

Just what he needed. No time to call Mickey and grab another hit. He'd have to do this one cold. "Shit."

Or would he?

Standing, he made his way towards the hallway in search of Graham. He was always good for a quick smoke, at least. As expected, his bodyguard sat outside, passing his time talking to one of the riggers.

"Hey, Gray! You got a minute?" Jake didn't wait for an answer. It was a rhetorical question.

"What's up?" Graham closed the door behind him, shutting out the rest of the entourage.

"I could use a smoke, but I just got called to stage. You got anything?" He spoke as he pulled a clean T-shirt over his head and pushed his feet into his boots.

Graham scanned the room, taking in the sight of the discarded small plastic bags and remains of white dust on the counter. "Do you think that's a good idea, considering you already had a date with Mickey today?" Graham's hands dug deep into his pockets, his fingers tracing the outline of a couple of smokes he had stashed away for later.

"You're not paid to think. Do you have anything or not?" Five years in the industry had allowed him to develop a take-no-prisoners attitude when he spoke to the people who worked for him. With everyone except Izzie. But then again, she was the one who kept him in work. For now, anyway.

Graham held out a lone roll-up for him, waiting until Jake had it between his lips before he ignited his lighter. Jake's eyes drifted closed as he inhaled deeply, allowing his lungs to absorb all they could before he slowly exhaled again. It wasn't his fix of choice these days, but it would take the edge off until he'd finished the gig.

"See, that wasn't so hard, was it?" He scowled before making his way out of his dressing room and down the rabbit warren towards the stage.

The gathered minions milled around, waiting as the support act finished their set. The young girl group were just emerging in the industry. Being on tour with Jake was going to have a huge impact on their career. The blonde one held Jake's interest more than the others. She took no crap from anyone from what he'd seen of her so far. Feisty to the core, precisely how he liked them.

"Don't even think it about it, Jake." The voice warned him from over his shoulder.

"Hey, you made it. I thought you were staying away tonight." Jake looked less than happy to have Izzie standing behind him.

"I'm pregnant, Jake, not ill. Besides, someone has to keep an eye on you. I hope you haven't tapped that." Izzie nodded her head towards the girls as they finished up on stage.

"Which one?" Jake's eyes flitted along the line-up of girls, his mind wandering to a level of depravity that made his cock twitch in anticipation.

"Jeez, Jake! Any of them. You need to stay away from them. I do not need you corrupting them or screwing with them, in any sense of the word. Understand?"

"Er, might be a tad late for that piece of advice. Sorry, Iz. I'll be good." Images from the previous night's hook up swarmed his brain, merging in to one awesome private video show. "Now, why don't you go home and put your feet up or something? I've got this." Leaning in, Jake planted a gentle kiss on her forehead. He owed everything he had achieved so far to this woman, and sometimes he forgot that. "Ben will be worried if he rings and you're not at home."

"Did I hear my name being bandied around? How you doing, man?" Ben's large hand grasped a firm hold of Jake's shoulder. "You look like shit. Are you... *wasted*?" Ben scrutinised Jake's face, scanning for some scrap of evidence.

"Hey! I thought you were out of town this weekend." Jake spoke whilst pulling Ben in for a man hug exchange as they always did, trying to diffuse the situation. "Great to see you. Nah, I'm just tired. You know how it gets." Turning his back on Izzie, he tried to ignore her glare as he focused on the roadies setting everything up for him. The last thing he needed before hitting the stage was another lecture from his manager.

"Jake, what the hell have you taken? Where the fuck is Graham? I warned him to keep that guy away from you." Izzie was all waving arms and fired up emotions as she scanned around them, trying to hunt down the bodyguard. "He's done. I'm done. I will not have him jeopardise your career anymore. God knows you can do that all by yourself. Can you get through the show? Jake, can you do the show tonight?" Izzie gripped his chin firmly in her hand as she stared angrily into his eyes, searching for the evidence she needed, some sign that he was coherent enough to perform.

"Yes. I told you, I'm fine. Quit stressing. I had one smoke. Nothing else, promise. I told you I'd quit and I did. I haven't seen Mickey for over a week. I'm done, Izzie. It's over. Now can I get on with what I'm supposed to be doing?" Jake gestured towards the stage as he tried to gently but firmly remove her hand from his face. "My world awaits!" With a quick wink in Izzie's direction and a pat on Ben's shoulder, Jake dashed out on stage to a crescendo of appreciative noise.

"Baby, he's good. He said so. You have to trust him. He's not a kid anymore. All this stress is not doing you or my offspring any good at all." Pulling Izzie into his chest, Ben could feel the tension rife throughout her body.

"You saw him, Ben. He is anything but fine. I don't trust him at all. How can I?" Pulling away from her husband, Izzie let out a long sigh. "I'm going to find Graham. I want to hear what he has to say. You stay here and enjoy yourself. I won't be long."

Reluctantly, Ben agreed. "Take it easy on him, baby. Jake's always been a loose cannon. It's not necessarily Gray's fault."

Somehow, he knew that had fallen on deaf ears.

CHAPTER
Two

"You're fired. Get your shit together and get out." Izzie didn't leave any time for explanations. "Andy!" She hollered down the corridor, and waited until the security guy's head popped out from the men's room door.

"Boss?" The huge, surly man emerged, his eyebrows were pulled in, reflecting his apprehension as he waited for Izzie to speak. The tone of her voice alone had alerted him to the fact that she didn't want him for a bit of friendly banter.

"Escort Graham off the premises, please. Make sure you remove him from all security software, change all passwords, and erase him from Jake's approved lists. He's to have no access to Jake whatsoever. Are we clear?" Izzie smiled sweetly at Andy, who she'd inadvertently promoted to head of Jake's security team.

"Sure thing, Izzie. You okay?" Andy looked a little bemused by the whole conversation.

"Hunky dory, Andy. Make sure his picture is removed from all access areas, too." Izzie turned her attention towards a stunned Graham, who stood with his mouth hanging open. Her eyes dropped to his Access All Areas pass that hung proudly around his neck. Graham's gaze lowered to Izzie's open hand. "Badge, car keys, and your Access pass, please." She held out her hand in front of her, waiting for Graham to hand everything over.

He pulled down hard on the lanyard that hung around his neck, the force causing the clasp to give way. "What the hell did I do? I haven't left him alone all day! I've sat outside his hotel room and his dressing room for fucking hours!" He bundled the keys and pass into Izzie's waiting hand.

"He's high as a fucking kite! That's what you did wrong. I told you to keep that piece of shit Mickey away from him. I warned you. I pay you to keep the scum away from him. Well, not anymore. Get out." The anger rolled off her in spades as she struggled to keep her cool. She knew all this stress was not good for her or the baby, but it came with the territory. Wherever Jake went, so did the stress.

Turning her back, Izzie headed into Jake's

dressing room. The sight that met her eyes shouldn't have been a surprise after seeing the state he was in, but it knocked her sick. Her stomach rolled, forcing her to head straight to the tiny bathroom and lose her dinner.

Once the retching had stopped, she entered the main room again, picking her way across the littered floor. Her eyes scanned the surfaces as she moved slowly, counting up the small clear plastic bags as she went. It was way worse than she'd first imagined. This was more than a bit of recreational usage. This was bad.

Out of desperation, Izzie pulled out her phone and scrolled through her contact list. There was only one person she needed to talk to right then.

"Tink! How's it going?" Alex's voice boomed in her ear. Once the lead singer of Uni-Fi, a hugely successful rock band, he was now enjoying success as a solo artist, but first and foremost, he was her brother.

"Hey. Not great, to be honest." Her emotions took a hold of her the second she heard her brother's voice. Fighting to control the wobbly lip and contain the tears, she took a deep breath.

"Is it the baby? Shit! I'm on my way, I'll book a flight." His voice grew muffled and she could barely make out the sounds of her brother talking to his girlfriend. "Okay, I'm back. Grace is looking for a flight now-"

"Alex! The baby is fine. I'm fine. It's Jake." Izzie heard him blow out a long breath as she began to tell him the whole messy story of how she was failing her artiste. Alex remained quiet and let her get it all out and off her chest.

"Iz, it's not your fault. He's an adult. You can't babysit him 24/7 and it sounds to me like he's simply lost his way a little. You can book him into rehab but he has to want to do it. I can get the number of the place Jez went to. It's supposed to be one of the best, but really, you have to get him to think it's his idea. He has to want this too, Izzie." Alex was always her "go to" person when she freaked out. His ability to calm her with a few simple words and brotherly support was exactly what she needed.

There was no way Jake would agree to rehab when he didn't think he had a problem. Looking around the room again, Izzie was unsure how this could be anything but a problem. After saying her goodbyes to her brother and promising to keep him updated, Izzie hit the contact list on her phone again.

Andy tapped lightly on the door and let himself in. "Ah, it all makes sense now." He spoke as he picked up one of the small empty plastic bags. "He's hitting it hard, isn't he? But to be fair, I'm not convinced that Gray was supplying him with any of this..." He indicated towards the devastation that was Jake's dressing room.

"I know that. But I warned him this would happen and not to let Jake out of his sight. He failed. His dealer got to him somehow, and seeing as he's the one I paid to keep him away, the responsibility ends with him."

Andy nodded as he sat down beside her. "Can't argue with that. Does Ben know you're in here? Want me to go grab him?"

"Nah, I'm good. I'll head back down there in a minute. Just got a phone call to make first." Izzie patted Andy's knee. "Thanks. I didn't mean to drop everything on you."

"No problem; only doing my job." Andy stood to leave. "I'll be outside. If you need anything, just shout."

Before the door had closed, Izzie was dialling again. Jake was her responsibility and no matter which way she looked at it, she'd failed him.

With all the arrangements in place, all that was left to do was convince Jake. Alex was right; he had to want to do this for himself.

"Izzie! Izzie! You'd better come see this..." Andy

threw the dressing room door open, panic imprinted on his face.

"What? What's he done now?" Izzie was used to Jake's antics; right from day one she'd had to keep him on a tight rein. One of her first jobs on meeting him had been to sort out the mess he and his former band mates had made at a hotel. They'd virtually wrecked the place. Setting fire to waste bins, destroying rooms and TVs. She'd seen the lot from him.

"He's getting pissed on stage. He's done two tracks and that's it. Ben's trying to coax him off now. The crowd are going mad. It's getting ugly. Someone threw a bottle of piss at him and he almost dived into the crowd to get at them. It's a fucking disaster." The security guard ran his hand through his hair, the exasperation marking his face. "I don't know what you want me to do…"

"Fuck! Get him off, now. I don't care if you have to drag him off kicking and screaming. Get him back here. I'll have someone call the police to manage the crowd clearing and I'll get someone from PR to sort out the backlash. And do me a favour. Keep Ben out of it, please." With no time to overthink it, Izzie headed into the corridor to help gather the rest of the security team. It was going to take more than Andy to drag Jake off stage.

Jake wasn't *built* by definition, but he was in good shape. Add that to the fact that he'd consumed a fair amount of alcohol and taken an obscene amount of shit; it wasn't going to be pretty. He'd put up a fight as he tried to prove his worth.

When Izzie reached backstage, the sight that greeted her was abysmal. Jake stood centre stage, his speech slurred as he addressed the violent crowd. "Wanker? Me? That what you called me?" Jake spoke slowly as he screwed up his eyes, trying to see past the first row of people. "Oh, I'm a wanker alright..." With the mic in one hand, he began to fumble with the fly on his jeans.

"Cut the fucking mic right now!" Izzie screamed over her shoulder into the maelstrom behind her. Bodies scrambled, voices shouted into walkie talkies, and three of the larger members of the security team rushed forward.

"Ah, shit! He's got his dick out. Lights! Cut the fucking lights!" Andy bellowed into his radio as he ran behind Ben onto the stage. It took six grown men to take Jake down. They even sat on him at one point, waiting it out until he stopped thrashing around and exhaustion took over.

Police swarmed the arena, clearing people out into the parking lot and ensuring they left the area. Izzie spoke with the officer in charge, assuring him a private ambulance was on its way and Jake would be checked into to a private facility that night. There was mention of indecent exposure charges as well as being drunk and disorderly. A whole shit storm swarmed in front of her. It was going to take some very carefully worded conversations to rescue this.

Her phone rang constantly with calls from the PR team, media, and everyone else who'd seen snippets of Jake's faux pas on the nightly news. Izzie dealt with them all, feeding them the line she wanted them to hear; *"Jake's been ill recently. He didn't want to let the fans down and wanted desperately to carry on with the schedule, despite doctors advising otherwise. He has been admitted to hospital tonight and at this time we have no further comment."*

As Olivia sat in the waiting room, her mind drifted to better days. Days when her life was far less complicated. To a time when all she had to worry about was the clothes on her back and being home in time for her curfew. Those days were long gone. No longer was there anybody sitting at home worrying about whether she'd arrive home safely or not. It was only Olivia now. Taking care of number one; that's all she had to think about.

Sometimes it bothered her, being alone, but most days she simply got on with it. What was the point in giving it too much brain space? She could take care of herself. Learnt how to be alone in the big wide world. The only thing she needed now was this job. The advert had been vague, but it did state the salary. And that was the very reason she was sitting there. The salary, and the fact that it required her to live-in, had been the biggest draw.

"Olivia Holmes?" A young woman peered from around the open door, a warm smile spread across her face as Olivia stood to greet her.

With her hand held out in greeting, Olivia addressed the woman, "Yes, hi. You must be Izzie?"

Izzie shook her hand briefly before scanning Olivia from top to toe. "That's me. Come on through." Standing to the side, she waved her into the office. The room was huge, with large floor to ceiling windows overlooking the city. Taking a seat in the chair Izzie had motioned to, Oliva gazed surreptitiously around the room. The bare brick walls were hung with industry awards and framed album cover artwork.

Shelves lined the wall behind her desk, each one heavy with photographs of Izzie with various bands and even more music awards.

"I'm sorry I kept you waiting but I was hoping Jake would be joining us for the interview. Sadly, he's been held up." Izzie smiled sympathetically at Olivia. "But then again, that's probably for the best."

"I don't mind waiting if he's on his way?" Olivia ran damp hands down the fabric of her trousers, smoothing out the imaginary creases and picking away at fluff that wasn't there. Deciding what to wear had been a difficult decision being more of a jeans and T-shirt girl, but she needed this job, so making a good impression pulled her in the direction of a kind of smart casual look. The clothes made Olivia uncomfortable. "I'm not in a rush, I mean."

"No, we'll just get started. He'd only be in the way. You'd be employed by me anyway, not Jake. Did you read the job description? Do you have any questions?" Izzie's eyes bore down on the young girl. "I'm assuming you've done your research and you know who you'll be working with. I'm also assuming you're intelligent enough to realise you can't believe everything the media print about him, too." She looked at Olivia pointedly, waiting for confirmation of both statements. Olivia nodded vaguely. Yes, she'd done the research, knew exactly who Jake Williams was. And yes, she wasn't naïve enough to believe everything written about him, but she also knew there was no smoke without fire. "You'd be required to accompany Jake wherever he went. Whenever he left the house. If he's awake, I'd expect you to be. He's not to be let out of your sight. At all. Would that be a problem?"

"I don't think so, no." The job description had sounded more like they were interviewing for a nanny or a babysitter. If the heading hadn't stated it was a live-in assistant job, she'd have questioned the listing in the advert.

"Jake has some…security issues, shall we say. It would be your job to keep me informed of anyone he has contact with, or any strange phone calls. Are you okay with that?"

"Excuse me for pointing this out, but I'm not a security guard, nor am I equipped to fight off an army of persistent female fans. If that's what you're looking for, then maybe I'm the wrong candidate…" There was no point in wasting either of their time if they needed a new member for the star's security team.

"That's not what I need from you. What I actually need is more of a… companion type figure. Someone who Jake can trust and feel comfortable with. But someone who's comfortable with letting me know when things get crazy. You're exactly what I'm looking for. Your reference from your last job states, and I quote, *'Takes no prisoners, speaks her mind, and is generally hard to sway.'* I'd say that pretty much covers everything Jake needs." The sickly sweet smile Izzie gave was unnerving.

"In my defence, my old boss was an arsehole. I'm not generally... difficult. So you want me to spy on him and report back to you? Am I right?"

"Well, not spy exactly. Your job would be to help keep him safe and on the right track. In return, you'd get to travel with him on tour, a decent salary, and a place to live. It's a pretty good deal." Izzie tapped her pen on the pad before her, weighing Olivia up with her steely stare as she thought over her words. "You'd get some down time, but to be honest, I'm paying pretty good money to get someone willing to put in the hours. Do you drive?"

The hours weren't a problem. Olivia was more than happy to work 24/7 if the pay was right, and it was. The idea of spying on her new boss, however, did not sit well; she did have some morals. "I have a full, clean licence, as stated on my application. How many others do you have to interview?" Olivia asked while mulling over her options.

"I saw two others this morning, but they were

flaky. And male. Jake would not be on board with this whole thing if I employed a bloke." Izzie sighed as she let the pen drop to the table. Leaning back in her chair, she studied the young girl carefully. "Olivia, the job's yours if you want it. It's not going to be an easy ride. Jake can be... challenging at times. But I think you're the girl to handle him. What do you say? We can set a settling in period, if that would make the decision easier for you. Say six weeks? Then, if you're really not happy, you can leave." She could see the cogs turning in Izzie's mind as she waited for a reply.

"Okay, I'll take it." How could she turn down the opportunity? "When do I start? I suppose I'll have to meet-"

The door to Izzie's office flew open and in bounced the man himself, rather like an over-excited puppy looking for its chew toy. Suddenly the room felt too small to accommodate three people.

"Hey, sorry I'm late. The driver never showed and then I couldn't find my phone to call a taxi and then this really great lyric came into my head; I had to write it down. You know how it is...oh, hi, sorry. Did I interrupt something here?" Jake ran his hand through his mop of hair, pushing it back from his face. He looked older than his twenty-two years, but that's what life in the fast lane did to you. Time in the spotlight had taken its toll on him.

"Jake, this is Olivia, your new assistant. You were supposed to be here this morning, and the driver *did* turn up, you sent him away. He rang me, so don't you lie to me." Izzie scolded the young star like he was some naughty child.

Walking around the large desk, Jake slung an arm around Izzie's shoulders before dropping a kiss into her hair. "Sorry, boss. I'm here now, though." His attention turned towards a startled Olivia. As his eyes began to wander down towards her boobs Olivia coughed politely, reminding him where his eyes needed to stay. "Olivia, you say? Can I call you Liv?"

"Not if you expect me to answer you, no."

"It sounds a little stuffy. Olivia." He tested every syllable as they rolled off his tongue. "I prefer Liv, less old person-y. We'll stick with Liv." Jake smiled sweetly as he rested his butt on the edge of Izzie's desk, his legs crossed at the ankles.

Rising from the chair, Olivia closed the short distance between them. With her hands on her hips, she addressed her new boss. "My name is Olivia. If you wish me to answer you, that's how you need to address me. Not Liv, Livvy, Oli or any other adaptation you decide to come up with, are we clear?"

Jake studied the way she looked with her head tilted to the side, her features set on her beautiful face. Her eyes, hard and staring, were glinting from the adrenalin that was obviously rushing through her veins. Yeah, he was certainly affecting her. "Ah, am I not the one paying your wages? Does that not give me any say here?"

"No." Olivia and Izzie spoke simultaneously.

"To both questions, Jake," Izzie said as she shuffled papers on her desk. "I'm paying Olivia's wages, so that makes me her boss, not you. So, in answer to your second question, you have zero say in anything." Izzie prodded him in the backside with the end of her pen. "Now, get your arse off my desk. There are enough chairs in here for you to sit on."

Grumbling, Jake moved to sit in a chair to the side of Olivia. It gave him enough leeway to admire the full package that was his assistant. He liked what he saw; everything from the way she wrinkled her nose as she concentrated, to the gentle tap of her foot as it rested against the chair leg. He could hear Izzie talking over contracts and shit, but he was more curious about what his new potential love interest had to offer him than talking over the finer details of a contract.

CHAPTER
Three

"Izzie, I've been home for ten days now. You don't need to stop by every day. Seriously, I'm fine." Jake sat at the breakfast bar in his kitchen, coffee cup cradled between his hands. It was just after ten in the morning and his manager had been there for what seemed like ages. Cedar Court had waved its so-called magic wand and returned Jake to them almost whole. He no longer needed a constant supply of white powder or booze to keep him on track, but in its place, he had developed a chain-smoking habit. The fact that he'd replaced one addiction with another didn't seem to bother him as much as it bothered those around him. What did bother him was Izzie wafting away the smoke he exhaled every ten seconds.

"Do you have to do that inside?" Izzie waved an arm in front of her face. It was a vain attempt at gaining some fresh, breathable air instead of rank cigarette smoke. "I'm here to make sure you haven't chased Olivia away. Where is she? I need to go over this week's schedule with her."

Appearing in the doorway, Olivia spoke. "I have Jake's schedule. You emailed it to me twice. I also have it on Jake's iPhone, complete with alarms and colour co-ordinated entries. Medical appointments are in blue, work appointments are in purple, and any meetings with you are marked in red. He's due in the studio in forty minutes." Olivia smiled smugly at Izzie. She may not have done this line of work before, but organisation was her middle name. She was self-labelled queen of the highlighter pen.

"Why am I in red?" Izzie leaned across to take in the wonder that was Olivia's online calendar. She didn't miss the quick alarmed glance Jake shot in the pretty young girl's direction.

Neither did Olivia, who immediately sprang to his rescue. "It was Jake's idea. The colour red makes him think of importance, so he suggested the colour for you so he'd know those meetings were crucial. The green blocks are when we work out." Olivia absently threw a jacket across the breakfast bar towards Jake. "Come on, hotshot. Time to go to work." With car keys swinging from her index finger, she left Jake and Izzie open-mouthed as she made her way towards the door.

"Work out?" They both asked simultaneously, ignoring the fact that she was ready to take him to the studio. The most Jake had ever worked out was pacing around on stage. That took the stamina of gods to keep up night after night on tour; it was the only exercise he regarded as necessary.

"Yep. Healthy body, healthy mind. We start tomorrow morning with a run at six." Olivia let the door shut behind her as Izzie smiled appreciatively.

"Erm, boss? This live-in assistant thing? Yeah, well, I really don't think it's gonna work. I mean, she's nice and everything, but I think you're wasting your money. I'm all good now. Fixed. The therapist said so. I just have to keep busy and we can do that without having somebody... Well, anyway, shall I tell her or will you?" Jake looked hopeful and ready to argue his case further. The text alert on his phone put an end to that.

'Do I have to come back in and get you? I don't do late, and neither do you now. Move it.'

Holding up his phone, he angled the screen in Izzie's direction, enabling her to read the message. He allowed the shrug of his shoulders to emphasise his point. Olivia had to go; there was no other way around it. He could not work with this annoying as hell girl. "See? She's a bully. I have ages to get to the studio. Why do I have to leave right now? We could leave in ten minutes and still get there with time to spare. If I start turning up early to shit then everyone is gonna think she has me whipped, which she totally hasn't, just for the record." The whine in his voice made him sound like a toddler throwing a tantrum.

Izzie laughed out loud. "What's wrong? Has she not succumbed to the charms of Little Jake yet?" His boss was finding it hard to control her laughter; it wasn't often that Jake came across someone who was immune to his kind of flirtation. "I like her. She stays. She's good for you."

"Izzie! Please. I'm clean and sober. Why do I need a babysitter? I don't want to do her kind of workout, and even if I did, it wouldn't be with her! I can think of much better ways to work up a sweat." Jake pouted, full lips thrust forward, forming an actual show of his lack of appreciation for his assistant. The new live-in arrangement had been in place for just over a week, and seriously, he didn't know how much more he could take of the ever-present, ever-eager Olivia. He'd caught her hovering outside his bathroom that morning while he'd been showering. After almost accusing her of being a peeping tom, they'd agreed he could have a few minutes alone whilst he washed. Although, she'd stipulated that any more than five minutes of bathroom time would earn him a stalking again.

There went his only bit of solitude.

His phone vibrated and danced along the breakfast bar. Olivia's name lit up the screen. "Look! She's fucking relentless. It starts at the ass crack of dawn and she doesn't stop until I'm passed out, exhausted from all her fucking interfering. I can't do this, Iz. Really, I can't." Jake slumped down onto one of the bar stools, his head rested in his hands as he waited for the phone to stop ringing. It didn't stop until Olivia's head popped around the doorframe.

"Jake, move it!" she ordered.

His backside left the stool in a heartbeat, and he grabbed his jacket and phone as he did. "Sorry. I was going over something with Izzie." His voice was barely above a murmur but his eyes shot to his manager's, his eyebrows raised almost to his hairline. "See what I mean?" he all but mouthed to Izzie.

"I think you'll live. You're a big boy, Jake. I'm sure you can handle a degree of light exercise and direction in your life." Izzie winked at him as she stood. Gathering her belongings, she followed them both out of the door. "Looks like you've got everything under control here, Olivia. I'm loving the take-no-prisoners attitude you have going on with our man here. Just what he needs. A little order and clarity in his life, don't you think?"

Jake almost baulked as his manager and his nemesis high-fived each other as they passed on the driveway. "Ladies, that's not even funny."

Opening the car door, Olivia slid in behind the wheel of the SUV, "I'm not laughing. Are you riding up front with me or hiding in the back like a sulky teenager?" She turned the key in the ignition and listened to the engine hum. Jake didn't answer, only slid into the seat behind his assistant and clicked his seatbelt in place. "Okay, Mr Sulky-pants, wave goodbye to Izzie." Olivia couldn't resist teasing him as she lifted her own hand to wave farewell to their boss as she manoeuvred the beast of a car out of the drive and out onto the main road. It was only the second time she'd driven him to the studio and the fourth time she'd driven the car at all. Slow and steady was the way forward. Jake's car was a long way from the heap of crap she was used to driving, and it now sat embarrassingly in Jake's driveway. It didn't matter if she pranged her own car; it had that many dings you'd be hard pressed to notice any new ones. Jake's car was different; it was brand spanking new and pristine. Inside and out. It even had that new car smell still.

CHAPTER
Four

*J*ake still had a week before he had to start back on his gruelling tour schedule. His *meltdown*, as it was being referred to, had put a temporary hold on all his planned appearances. They'd had to be rescheduled at the end of the tour, but next week he was due to fly out to Germany to pick up where he'd left off.

Everyone around him was feeling the strain. Not only from rehearsals, but from stepping on eggshells around Jake. For the last three days his mood had been blacker than black. The best part of the last twenty-four hours had seen him holed up in his room, picking out tunes on his guitar. Every time Olivia made any attempt at extracting him from his pit, he hunkered down even more. Up until an hour ago, his door had at least remained unlocked. She'd been allowed to pass him food and drink as and when he requested, but now it was locked. He'd informed her it would remain that way until she saw the light and quit her so-called job.

"Gee, thanks, Jake." Olivia stood stoically outside his door "I have a key. If you don't open up and come out here, I'm coming in. Or calling Izzie. Take your pick."

"You wouldn't fucking dare!"

Images of Jake either drunk or worse flashed through her mind. She hadn't left him alone at all, but she knew he had connections. If he wanted a drink that bad, he'd find a way. And that meant her job was on the line. If Izzie found out Jake was drunk or high, she'd sure as hell fire her. Jake knew that. He also knew Olivia was aware of that fact too. Addicts were known for hiding the goods in unsuspecting places. Olivia made a mental note to check every inch of his room when she finally gained access again. She'd have no option but to use the key she'd found. Taking a deep breath and steadying herself for whatever version of Jake she was about to find on the other side of the door, she slid the key into the lock and turned it.

Cracking the door open slightly, she spoke to announce her intention to enter the room. "You left me no choice..." She was hoping the worst she'd encounter would be a pissed off rock star. What she didn't expect was the glass that hurtled across the room and smashed against the wall less than a foot away from her face. She didn't recognise the scream that echoed around the room as her own until she realised the laughter was coming from Jake.

"Get the fuck out of my room. My room is off limits. Unless you're naked and invited, neither of which you are." The words were ground out spitefully.

"You throw anything else at me ever again, Jake, and I swear I'll rip your fucking head off your fucking shoulders and shove it so far up your arse you'll need a whole army to get the fucking thing back out. Are we clear?" Olivia tried, unsuccessfully, to keep her voice calm and even in tone as she sidestepped the broken glass.

Jake glowered from where he sat on his bed, his guitar by his side. Notepaper lay strewn across the crumpled sheets. Most of it had a single line written on it at the most. Olivia's eyes scanned the floor around the bed, searching for signs of his drinking amongst the screwed up pieces of paper. Moving nearer to the waste bin, Olivia risked a glance inside, checking for empty bottles or signs of his drug habit. She saw nothing of alarm but then realised the waste bin was too obvious; she'd need to up her game.

"You won't find anything," he stated, more calmly than he had been minutes previously.

"Is that because you've hidden the evidence or because you have nothing to hide?" Wide eyes scanned every surface of the room. Nothing was out of place except the shattered glass.

"Fuck off, Liv."

"No. And it's Olivia, remember?" When Olivia had taken this job, she knew it wouldn't be a walk in the park. She knew exactly who Jake Williams was, having followed his career for the past few years. Maybe even fantasized a little about him if truth be told, but the man who sat before her was so far removed from the well put together rock star show pony his adoring fans were so used to seeing. Instead, Jake seemed all too human. He was barely dressed, wearing a pair of old joggers with his bare feet jutting out from the cuffs at the bottom. What was it about men's feet that made them so damned sexy? His hair was unwashed and fell flat against the angles of his face. The three day old scrub that scattered his jawline made him look dirty and unkempt. On anyone else it may have looked sexy, but on Jake, it didn't work.

"What's going on, Jake?" Olivia gently questioned.

"Working, what does it look like?" The retort was angry.

"It looks like a mess to me." Slowly, she made her way towards where Jake sat, carefully picking her way through the broken glass on the floor as she went. He pulled his legs in closer to his body, wrapping his arms around his knees where he rested his chin.

"Fuck off, Liv. I want to be alone right now."

She sighed. "Olivia, not Liv."

"Fuck. Off." Maybe aggravating him and pushing the name issue while he was in this mood wasn't her finest idea.

"You're due at the studio in an hour. I'm going to make you something to eat, then I can clean up this mess and then we're leaving." If she gave him fair warning of what was expected of him, he usually responded well, but not this time. He didn't answer, only stared out into nothingness before him. Olivia moved into the space directly in front of the star, repeating what she'd told him.

"I hate it when you use that voice. Reminds me of being in therapy. Can you just be normal? Like, talk to me like I'm normal, just for once." Jake grabbed the guitar from beside him, pulling it into his lap. Olivia flinched slightly, unsure if he was about to throw that next. He didn't, he simply held it close to his chest as though it provided him with some comfort.

"You threw a glass at me. Now you want a normal

conversation? I don't feel much like being in the same room as you, never mind talking to you." Turning on her heels, Olivia headed for the bedroom door. "Your lunch will be ready in five minutes." She thought better of closing the door behind her. With it open, she could just about hear him moving around while she was in the kitchen. It gave her a slight bit of control over the otherwise fraught situation.

Just over five minutes later, Jake appeared in the kitchen doorway. His joggers had been swapped for a pair of designer jeans, and his hair had been slicked back with whatever product he favoured. His feet, however, were still bare, the left one bleeding slightly.

"I stepped on some of the broken glass." He looked forlornly at the foot he'd raised from the floor. "Do I have a first aid kit anywhere?" His eyes never met Olivia's, instead they remained fixed on the slow trickle of blood that emerged from right below his toe.

"Did you get all the glass out? Come here. I'll clean it up for you." She indicated to the barstool, patting the seat with her hand as she fished around in the first aid box for tweezers and something to cover the area with.

Jake hobbled across the room, leaving spots of blood on the bright white tiled floor. "Sorry. For throwing the glass, I mean. I wouldn't have hit you with it." Jake positioned himself comfortably on the barstool, his injured foot rested across his knee as Olivia tended to the small, almost insignificant cut. "I was only letting off steam. I would never hurt you."

"Most people go for a run or work out, go for a walk, or use a punch bag to let off steam. They don't throw glasses at other people's heads." Running an alcohol wipe across the open wound, Olivia pressed hard to stem the bleeding. She struggled to hold in the giggle as Jake flinched in pain when she sterilised the wound. "You want to talk about it?"

"No. What I want is a drink."

"Not happening, Jake."

"Please. Just one. I write better when I've had a drink. If I turn up today with nothing then I'm done. They won't renew my contract, I'll be out of work, you'll be out of work. It's a vicious circle. You want to ruin my career over just one drink?" His puppy dog eyes sought out Olivia's icy blue ones.

Olivia could feel his eyes boring holes into the side of her head as he spoke. She avoided any eye contact with him. "I'm never going to supply you with booze, Jake. Please don't ask me again."

"I'll stop again tomorrow. It's only one drink," he said, his voice coarse. "Just get me something."

"I'm not getting you alcohol." Olivia straightened,

admiring her handiwork on his foot. "Or anything else. Izzie would kill me." Packing the first aid kit away, she busied herself to avoid further discussion about becoming Jake's supplier.

"She won't know. It'll be our secret. Come on, it's one drink. Then I'll finish the song, you can drive me to the studio, and I'll never touch another drop. Promise." Jake's eyes sparkled as he tried to tempt his assistant over to the dark side.

"Eat your lunch. I'll grab you a shirt. Then we'll head to the studio. That's all that's on offer, sorry." Olivia moved out of his way, making her way out of the kitchen and up to Jake's bedroom. She could hear him cursing as he opened cupboards and drawers while she rummaged through the rails of clothes. It would have been easy to give in to him, provide him with the drink he thought he needed, but then what next? Because she was damned sure there'd be a next time.

It wasn't until she made her way back out of the bedroom that she noticed the broken glass had been cleared from the bedroom floor. All that remained was a few shards that she carefully avoided, making a mental note to vacuum when they got back later.

Handing the shirt over to Jake, she noticed a small cut on the palm of his hand. "You need me to look at that too?" Olivia took his hand in hers to examine the damage further.

"No. It's barely a nick. It's not even bleeding. Nothing to worry about." Jake ran his fingertip over the small mark on his palm.

"Thank you for clearing up the glass, Jake."

"Sorry I broke it in the first place."

CHAPTER Five

The studio was quiet. The whole place had been booked out for Jake. It helped that Izzie and her hugely famous husband owned it. They'd started their own business after they got married. Izzie had been in a nasty car accident which had left her uncertain about her career in the industry, but with Ben's support and gentle encouragement, they'd built a very successful talent management business. Izzie Mitchell was responsible for a lot of the current chart topping bands and actively sought out new and upcoming talent. She managed not only Jake, but Ben and her own brother, Alex, too.

She was a force to be reckoned with. Inside the industry, her name was synonymous with success. The amount of unsolicited submissions the company got daily was ridiculous. There was a constant stream of wannabe bands and solo artistes trying to impress the industry's finest. But Izzie was picky. She had to be, in order to maintain her reputation of being the best of the best. She didn't shy away from telling someone they were crap. The majority of the talent submissions never got a call back, they merely disappeared into oblivion after she or her team had heard the first line or opening chords. Only the truly gifted were granted a meeting.

Lounging on the plush sofa, Olivia flicked through magazine after magazine while Jake sat inside the soundproofed recording booth. She could watch him through the window as, time and time again, he went over the same few lyrics, putting a different spin on them sometimes. The guys in the small room off to the left of where Olivia sat fiddled with sliding buttons and knobs, repeatedly speaking to Jake, asking him to try different versions of the same words.

When boredom really set in, she picked up her phone and started up the calendar app. No harm in making sure all the arrangements were watertight for the next week's schedule. As she scrolled through the next day's appointments, the door swung open and in walked Izzie with two large takeout coffee cups balanced in a cardboard carrier in one hand and a paper bag from Martha's Deli in the other.

"Figured coffee and cake wouldn't go amiss?" Izzie

dropped down onto the sofa next to Olivia, placing the hot drinks on the table before offering the bag to the young girl. "Wasn't sure which your favourite was so I picked out a few. Take your pick. I like them all." Izzie rubbed her hand against her swollen pregnant stomach. "I think this baby is going to come out addicted to Martha's."

Olivia sniggered as she peeked inside at the donuts and delicious cake selection that called to her. "That's not a bad thing. And I'm sure I read somewhere that cake contains zero calories to pregnant women. It would definitely be too mean otherwise."

"Don't tell me that or I may just eat the one I was planning on saving for Jake, too." Once Olivia had decided on the donut, Izzie tucked into the carrot cake slice. "Martha makes the best frosting. I made Ben beg her for a tub of the frosting on its own last week. He's going to have to roll me into the delivery suite if I carry on eating at this rate."

"Stop. You can barely tell you have a baby in there. You have nothing to worry about, and if a pregnant lady can't eat an occasional treat, well, what's the point?" The words came out mumbled around the donut she'd almost inhaled.

Izzie only grunted around her last mouthful of cake; it was too good to risk losing a crumb to speech.

They sat in companionable silence as they drank and watched Jake work for a few minutes.

"How's he holding up? He looks tired." Twisting in her place, Izzie studied Olivia, waiting for her to respond.

"He's not great today. He's more distant and definitely more objectionable." She toyed with the idea of retelling the broken glass story but thought better of it. That was best put to bed and forgotten about. Nobody died. "The realisation of getting back on tour next week has hit him, I think."

"Are you coping with him? Do you need anything? He has to get back to work, sadly. I've held it off for as long as I could. Once he's done the four Germany dates, he's back in London for the last leg of the tour. Home dates are always easier. I have no idea why but Ben and Alex say the same thing too. Must be a bigger adrenalin high or something." Sipping on the hot drink, Izzie turned her attention towards her artiste, studying him as he moved one half of the headphones away from his left ear. Nodding towards him, she smiled as she spoke again. "Alex does that. With the headphones. He never sits with both over his ears either. He swears they inhibit his performance in the booth. Jake idolises my brother, still."

Olivia smiled as she watched the pride in Izzie's

eyes. "He's more than a pay cheque to you, isn't he? I can see it, the way you look at him with more than a boss' eyes. He's so much more to you, isn't he?"

"They all are. Each and every person I've signed is important to me, and for so much more than what they can earn for me. But yeah, you're right, Jake's different. He's like family to me. A kind of annoying younger brother, one that I spend half my life wanting to kill and the other half wanting to smother with unconditional love." Chuckling, Izzie turned her attention back to Olivia. "Don't tell him that, though. He really doesn't need the extra ego boost. He's bad enough on his own."

"I think he knows it deep down, I just think he's forgotten it along the way. I think he's forgotten a lot of the good things about himself and those closest to him. That's half his problem. The bad stuff has kind of taken over the good bits." Olivia gazed at her charge through the glass, admiring him at his work. His tantrum from that morning was probably forgotten as far as he was concerned. The tension that had been evident on his face when they first arrived had disappeared. He was in the zone. Work soothed him, and it was obvious. What wasn't obvious was exactly how he was going to cope back out in the real world when the tour resumed next week. Jake must have felt her eyes on him. He slipped the headphones from his ear and let them rest around his neck. He offered her a meek, almost apologetic smile, before running his hand through his hair and pushing it back. The same action she'd watched him do hundreds of times, only somehow it now seemed more significant. It made him appear far more vulnerable than she'd ever realised him to be. Her heart did a funny little clenching thing.

Picking up on the knowing looks that passed between Olivia and Jake, Izzie scowled, her eyes narrowing as she searched both their faces for any guilty tell-tale signs. "Has something happened that I should know about?" Her gazed flicked backwards and forwards between the two.

"Like what? He hasn't had a drink or scored if that's what you mean." The memory of the morning's spat with Jake sprang to Olivia's mind. She was absolutely certain beyond all doubt, well maybe not *all* doubt, but pretty sure, that Jake hadn't had a drink or been wasted. At no point could he have possibly had access to anything.

"Okay... and you and Jake are getting along?" Izzie's eyes narrowed into slits as she studied Olivia's face closely, looking for any tell-tale signs.

"Well, that would be stretching the truth a touch, but we haven't tried to kill each other yet." Not if you didn't count the flying glass. "It's early days. He's still getting used to me being around 24/7 so yes, we're co-existing just fine."

"Good, because it'll be worse when you're in Germany next week. He'll be even more intolerable once the stress levels soar. You're going to have to try and keep him out of trouble and entertained. Boredom is a trigger for Jake. Keep him busy and that's half the battle." Digging around in her bag, Izzie produced her phone. Making a few tapping motions, she opened up her emails. "I've sent you all the final travel arrangements, hotel bookings, and everything you'll need for Germany. Did you bring your passport?"

Olivia handed over her passport. She hadn't really travelled anywhere alone. Not that she'd be alone next week - Jake and his whole entourage would be with them - but the only time she'd ever left the country before had been with her family before everything went belly up. This was a new venture for her, and not only would she have to take care of herself, she'd be required to look after Jake too. Ensuring his safety and security needs were met at all times would be paramount. Izzie had drilled that into her already. There would be the task of getting him through the airport unscathed then onto the plane. The flight itself was the easy part as far as she could see. At least he couldn't abscond once they were airborne.

"Everything's in place for you. The driver will collect you both in the morning, he'll drop you straight on the runway next to the private jet where you'll need to board the plane. I'll hand all the passports and documentation over to them now, so you'll have nothing to worry about on the day." Izzie's gaze remained locked on her emails as she spoke. "The security team should be already on board by the time you arrive."

Perhaps there was no need to get stressed out after all.

"You mean I won't have to get Jake through the airport or check-in?" The relief was almost evident on Olivia's face. Getting Jake into the car and then back out again at the airport should be pretty easy.

"No." Izzie giggled. "Jake stopped doing that a while ago. It's too risky. He gets mobbed, which isn't pleasant for anybody. Andy will be at the plane to meet you, just in case there is the odd errant fan, but to be honest, you should sail through." Packing everything back in her bag, Izzie looked warily at Olivia before she continued. "I've made sure that there'll be no alcohol served on board for the flight, but someone will sneak some on. Everyone knows to keep it away from Jake. I want to know, the second you land, who takes it on board." It was a command not a request. "I will not have anyone working around Jake that cannot or will not take his health seriously, okay?"

"Goes without saying. Although from what I've seen of the team, they're pretty tight knit and care about him, so it should all be fine." Olivia could only hope. The last thing she needed was to have to shop one of the team. That wasn't part of her life plan for making friends.

"I love your naiveté, I really do. A few more weeks in this industry should see that knocked right out of you, sadly. Anyway, I have to dash. I'll speak to you soon. Any questions, ring me." Standing up, Izzie made her way over to the sound booth, cracked the door open slightly and said her goodbyes to Jake before leaving the studio and a rather bemused Olivia behind.

CHAPTER
Six

*A*fter hours in the studio watching Jake work, Olivia was more than ready to go when he finally emerged from the booth, a little tired and unsteady. He looked drained, which confirmed Olivia's fears that the gruelling schedule that stretched out before him for the next couple of weeks was going to make their life difficult.

"All done?" Standing, Olivia moved around the small table towards Jake and the doorway, watching him lift his arms above his head as he stretched out some of the stress from the day. She could sense the tension in him. "You got a knot you can't reach there? Here, turn around."

Jake spun around, presenting his back to her. Rolling his shoulders, he elongated his arms in front of his chest. "It's right underneath my left shoulder blade. Just can't loosen it." Olivia set her thumbs to work, kneading and massaging his muscle, allowing her fingers to dig deep and release the tension knot she could feel. "Argh, yeah, right there. Fuck, that feels epic."

"Good. Not too much?" Olivia peered on tiptoes over his shoulder to check he wasn't in any pain.

"Nah, go harder. Fucking hell, you've got magic fingers." Jake's body relaxed underneath her touch.

"It sounds like some kind of porno out here. Would you two get a room?" Greg emerged from behind his mixing desk, chuckling. "Great work today, Jake. Keep that up and you're going to kill it next week." Man hugs and back slapping ensued as the two large men congratulated each other on the great things they'd achieved during their time together.

Turning his attention back to Olivia, Jake motioned towards the door. "Home it is then, to carry on this porno, Liv."

"It's Olivia. And in your dreams, Jake." She sniggered as she led the way out towards the car park. As the glass doors swung open, a loud screech rang through her ears. At first sound, it could have been mistaken for an animal, but there were words mixed within the hysteria. "Is that a girl?" Olivia asked.

"What the hell?" Greg rushed passed her scarcely in time to grab Jake and put himself between the screaming banshee and the star. Jake hardly blinked, standing there dazed as the girl who looked about eighteen years old fought furiously to get past Greg to her idol. Luckily, Greg stood firm, not granting the girl any access. Olivia's brain kicked into gear and she rushed to Greg's side, presenting a wall for Jake to stay behind.

His head bobbed out between those of his two defenders, addressing his fan. "If she wants an autograph, that's cool. I'll sign her tits or whatever it is she wants signing." The cheeky wink he gave the girl only served to fuel her thriving need to get to him.

"See, he said it's fine! He said he'd sign these puppies." Promptly, Olivia was faced with the girl's breasts, pushed up proudly in a barely concealing bra. "I love you, Jake!" she shouted past Greg and Olivia, who continued to try and put some distance between Jake and the fan.

"He's not deaf. Stupid maybe, but not deaf. Put them away, darling." With her arms crossed over her chest, Olivia belittled the fan.

"She doesn't need to put them away; they're pretty impressive. I mean, have you got a pen, gorgeous?" Fighting his way past his protectors, Jake emerged triumphant with the biggest smirk on his face.

"Move, bitch!" The girl snarled at Olivia. If she'd

frothed at the mouth like a rabid animal, nobody would have been surprised. Her smile turned sickly sweet as the object of her desire took the pen she'd found and scribbled his name across the ample flesh on show. "I'm going straight to get it tattooed now. It'll look amazing." Her eyelashes batted longingly at Jake as she tucked her boobs back inside her top. "I'll show you the finished result, if you like. Just me and you. Just say when and where." The girl was rising up to almost hysteria again as she realised her time with Jake was coming to an end.

"I don't think so. He's busy." Olivia dismissed the girl as she clicked the button on the key fob to open the car. "Get in the car, Jake." Greg stood aside to open the door for him.

"You fucking bitch! You're only jealous." As Olivia turned her back, the fan threw herself towards the car and Jake. Her arms flailed as she tried to grasp any part of Jake she could. In a split second, Jake was clutching one hand to his cheek and the other was held in front of him, trying to stop the girl advancing any further. Blood trickled down his cheek, causing Olivia to see red. Anger thundered through her, forcing her body forwards and in front of Jake.

With her body wedged between Jake and the fan, her face glowed purple with rage. "Get the fuck away from him. Now!" Without hesitation, Olivia shoved the girl hard in the middle of the chest. She obviously hadn't been expecting it. The girl went sprawling backwards, landing with a cold hard thump on the tarmac. "Fangirl down. *Fangirl down.*" Olivia laughed as she turned her attention back to Jake. "Let me see." She lifted his hand away from his face, revealing a long gash and a second minor graze to his cheek. "We better get you home and that cleaned up."

Jake nodded in agreement then held his hand up to high-five his PA. "Did you really say '*fangirl down*'? That was awesome."

"I'll sue you, just you watch," the girl screamed at Olivia as she picked herself up from the dirty car park floor. "I can sue for damages."

"Yeah? Well, let's see. I have blood dripping down my face from an unprovoked attack after I signed your fucking saggy tits. I think I'm the one who can sue for damages. My eyes will never be the same again after seeing those things. Go home." Jake shut the car door, but only after he'd made sure Olivia had climbed in the front and shut hers first.

They both watched from the safety of the car as Greg escorted the girl out of the car park. "It'll be worse after next week," Jake muttered from behind Olivia.

Her heart pounded inside her chest. It felt like it was trying to break free from the confines of her ribcage. That was just one girl. She'd yet to experience the full on hysteria that was sure to follow Jake everywhere he went. She'd had it pretty easy so far. They'd only really travelled between the studio and his home, where the only people they'd encountered had been studio staff or Jake's neighbours, neither of which were impressed by the star. Being on tour with him was going to bring thousands more girls just like that one, all throwing themselves at him, all wanting to take home a piece of him as a keepsake.

She had a feeling her job was about to get a lot more complicated.

"Does it not piss you off? All that attention and being mauled all the time? Must get pretty boring after a while." Olivia glanced at Jake through the rear view mirror. "I bet even the sex gets shitty too. I mean, it must be like performing on stage, only you're in a bed naked and not in front of thousands of people."

"You've never had sex with me. It's never boring and it rarely happens in bed. Granted, it isn't normally in front of thousands either, although if you ask Izzie, she'll tell you it nearly was." Jake chuckled reflectively at the memory of his last gig and the absolute fuck up that it was. "Yeah, that wasn't my finest moment."

"I heard. That's all behind you now, though, right?"

"Guess so." Jake rested his head against the back seat, his eyes closed as he spoke. "I hope it is but I have to take this one day at a time. But I'm not gonna lie, it kinda feels like a part of me is missing now. The part that used to kick back and enjoy life seemed to go hand in hand with the coke and drink. With a few JDs inside me, I'd have had that girl in the back of the car and back at the house before I'd even thought about it. Not anymore."

To anyone else, he would have looked bored, but the way he worried away at his fingernails gave him away; he wasn't nearly as unaffected by titty girl as he was trying to make out. Olivia was learning to see right through him and his nuances.

"I feel kind of responsible for that little... performance." Olivia ran her hand through her long hair as she checked Jake in the rear view mirror again. "I'm employed to take care of you. I'm supposed to stop people like that getting to you. Izzie is going to kill me when she sees your face."

"That wasn't your fault. You couldn't have stopped that. You're not employed as security, you're my PA, my right hand woman. The person that stops me getting shit-faced." Digging inside his pocket, Jake pulled out his cigarettes, placing one between his lips. "Do you mind?"

Olivia shook her head as she slowed to stop at a red light. "I don't think Izzie will see it like that."

Taking a long draw on the cigarette, Jake allowed the calm to spread through his body as he inhaled further. "I'll speak to her, don't worry. Anyway, you put that girl on her arse which was epic. Did you see her face? Pure rage."

Leaning forward, Jake held his hand up to high-five her again. "Come on, Liv. Don't leave me hanging,"

"It's Olivia," she said as she slapped her hand against his.

CHAPTER
Seven

*L*owering the lid on the toilet, Olivia waved him over. "Sit on the edge of the seat," she instructed.

Jake's en-suite was huge, larger than the family bathroom she'd had to share when she was growing up. There were three other bathrooms in Jake's house, not including the one downstairs. She hadn't been so lucky growing up; she'd even had to share a bedroom with her sister up until leaving home. The space available to her now felt almost too much to handle. It made her feel vulnerable and exposed.

Opening the first aid box she'd grabbed from the kitchen, she removed the alcohol wipes and began cleaning up the wound on Jake's face. She'd need to replace them; there'd be none left after cleaning him up again. Her fingers worked diligently, wiping over the abrasions on his cheek. "This might sting a bit but I don't want it getting infected. I dread to think where her hands have been." Olivia shuddered at that thought.

"I could just wash my face. Good old soap and water never did anyone any harm. It's not that bad, is it?" Jake squirmed sideways, trying to catch a glimpse of his reflection in the mirror.

"Will you hold still? If it isn't properly cleaned it will leave a scar on that beautiful face of yours." Gripping his chin in her thumb and forefinger, Olivia pulled him back to face her. "I think your T-shirt is ruined. Sorry."

Glancing down, Jake saw the drops of blood splattered on the front of him. "Aw, shit. I love this shirt. It's my favourite." He pouted.

"I'm sure you have others. Like racks and racks of others. I've seen them. It's just a T-shirt." Taking a step back, Olivia admired her handiwork. Once cleaned up, Jake's face didn't look nearly as bad as she'd first thought it would. Perhaps Izzie would never notice. Well, maybe if he walked sideways until it healed. "I think you'll do."

"Thanks." Twisting his head from side to side, he admired his reflection in the mirror. "So, you think I'm beautiful? I didn't realise you liked me even a tiny bit," Jake teased.

"What?" Confusion etched on her face as her cheeks flushed at his words.

"You said I'd have a scar on my *'beautiful'* face if you didn't clean it up. You said it." He laughed as Olivia's cheeks glowed pink.

"Well, I've seen much worse. You're not so bad, I suppose. For an ex-boy-band-wannabe-rock-star," she teased him back.

She turned her attention back to the first aid box, repacking it and tucking it away in the bathroom cupboard. Jake watched her from his position on the closed toilet seat lid. "Look, about today. I want to apologise again, for the glass and the fucking fan. Both were my fault and you were in the firing line. Your job... it shouldn't put you in the firing line twice in one day. So, thanks. You know, for looking after me."

Her heart did that funny clenching thing again. He really did her head in most of the time with his unreasonable demands and his bad attitude towards her, but now she'd seen a different side to him. A side she much preferred. One she could get used to spending time with.

"Apology accepted, and you're welcome. I'm glad I was there to help. It was kinda fun seeing her sprawled out on the floor. I've never put anyone on the floor before." Olivia chuckled as she recalled the girl's indignant face.

He looked up at her, his eyes mellow for a change. "Sure was." He smiled softly. For a moment they stared at each other in silence, like they were waiting for something, or trying to figure something out. Then Jake turned away, breaking the moment. "Shall I order a takeaway? We could watch that Deadpool movie you've been going on about. I bought it, thought we could see what all the fuss is about. It's not my normal type of movie but you've not shut up about it so I thought we could give it a go together. If you want to."

"Wow, Ryan Reynolds and an apology all in the same day. What more could a girl want?"

"You wound me. I'm hurt beyond all recognition." Jake clutched his hands to his chest in simulated pain. "I try to do a good thing and there you go, mocking me. I'll eat curry alone. You can sit in your room and do whatever it is you do in there. Paint your nails or something." He pushed his lips out in a fake pout to show his displeasure at her teasing. "I think if we go over your contract, I'm pretty sure it says you have to be with me whenever I'm awake. I could even get Izzie to fire you."

"You'd miss me if I went." A small part of Olivia held on to the hope that he'd tell her she was right, that he would miss her presence in his life. "Besides, you never mentioned curry. I'm in. I'll put the movie on, and you order the curry. Just let me put some PJs on first. Meet you downstairs in five." As she headed out of the bedroom, she called back over her shoulder towards the bathroom to where Jake was scrolling through his phone. "Order some nibbles too. You can't have curry without the bhajis."

Twenty minutes later, Olivia walked into the large lounge area. Jake had drawn the curtains and set out plates and cutlery on the low coffee table. Scatter cushions were thrown on the floor, ready for her to sit on, and the tin foil takeaway dishes waited unopened on a tray. On the massive TV screen, the movie was paused and ready to play. "There you are. I thought you'd had second thoughts and fallen asleep."

"Sorry. I grabbed a quick shower. What did you order?" Lifting up the edges of the boxes, Olivia peeked inside, trying to guess what they held.

Jake laughed as Olivia tried to peel the lids open without burning her fingertips. "I wasn't sure what you liked, so I ordered a few main dishes for you to choose from and most of the side dishes on the menu. Dig in. We can share." He handed her a plate before opening up all the miniature tin foil containers for her.

Settling in on a cushion next to Jake felt like the

most natural thing in the world to do. She wasn't sharing dinner with a rock star, she was having dinner with a friend. Or at least that was how it was beginning to feel. They were settling into a comfortable tolerance of each other. The fact that she could feel his body heat from the short distance between them raised her own temperature slightly, not to mention the effect it was having on her heart rate too. What the hell had gotten into her recently was anybody's guess. She needed this job. She didn't need any added hassle that came with being even slightly attracted to Jake. This new heightened awareness of him was a touch scary to say the least. Maybe it was because of all the drama the day had brought their way. From the throwing of glasses and trying to mortally wound her, to Olivia defending him against a crazy fan, the day had been a wave of emotional highs and lows. No doubt the next day they'd go back to normal, with Jake ignoring her for the best part of the day.

The time for freaking out about what may or not be feelings for Jake was not now. There'd be plenty of time for that later.

CHAPTER Eight

"Why do you keep staring at me like that? I thought you wanted to watch this film, or perv over Mr Reynolds." Jake's eyes never left the large screen as he spoke. The film had been on for over an hour and had failed to hold Olivia's attention.

"What?" asked Olivia in a confused voice. "I'm not staring at you."

"Yes, you are. You've been doing it for the last hour. You have no clue what's going on in this film, do you?"

"It's all in your imagination. Of course I know what's going on."

Jake wasn't imagining anything. For some reason, she couldn't take her eyes off him. Not even the hot Hollywood A-lister on the screen could hold her interest. Somehow, after the day they'd had, everything seemed different. The fact was, that idiotic clenching thing her heart kept doing was just too stupid for words. Whatever it took, she'd have to get it under control.

"Do you want me to turn it off? If you're not enjoying it, I mean." Jake turned his head to face her. "I bought it because you've mentioned it a hundred times in the last few days. I don't mind."

"Relax, I'm enjoying it. It's a great film. You're missing all the good bits." Olivia tipped her chin in the direction of the screen as the action played out before them.

Turning back around to watch the movie, Jake slid further down into the pile of cushions, wiggling as he got comfortable again. "Well, try to watch the film then, and not me. It's making me uncomfortable."

Olivia wrapped one of the throw blankets around herself, clutching it to her chest as a comforter and a kind of barrier between Jake and her. The fear that he could hear the effect he was having on her had become too much in the small space between them. The protection the blanket offered her was more than welcome.

"Are you cold?" he quizzed.

"No. Why?"

Jake let his head roll slowly sideways to take in the

full view of her. As his eyes wandered the full length of her, they appeared somewhat unfocused. "The blanket. You're hanging onto it like your life depends on it. I thought you were trying to keep warm. If you're cold, I can switch the heating on."

"Oh, no. I'm fine. It's in case there's any gory bits. In the film. I'm not good with blood and guts," she lied. The blanket was her armour. There to protect her from all things Jake related.

The cheeky laugh that escaped him was enchanting. The sound enveloped her like a soft, warm blanket. He hadn't laughed much in the last few days; it was a small glimpse of the old Jake shining through. "If it gets scary, you could always scoot over here. I can protect you from the nasty men on the screen. Better than that old thing could, anyway."

"Yeah, no thanks. I think I'll take a rain check on that offer, Mr Williams." Although, Olivia's heart was begging for a different conclusion. One that involved lots of bodily contact and limbs entwined in a hot heap. Maybe even slightly glistening skin thrown in for good measure. What the hell was wrong with her?

"Well, don't say I didn't offer. Maybe after this we can watch a horror movie. You'll want me to protect you then, I bet." Jake waggled his eyebrows up and down suggestively as a grin spread from ear to ear.

"Over my dead body! I wouldn't sleep for a week if you made me watch a horror movie." Olivia shuddered at the thought, goosebumps spreading over her arms. They sat in relative silence, studying the movie for a while, with the exception of Olivia, who studied her crush slyly every now and again.

As the credits rolled, Olivia turned to speak to Jake, only to realise he was asleep. His head lolled backwards onto the sofa where his back had been rested for the last two hours. A small amount of drool slipped from between his lips and dribbled down his chin. Olivia watched as it traced its way over the stubble which was starting to appear across his jaw. A small wet patch had formed on the sofa just beneath his cheek; he'd obviously been asleep a while. It seemed a shame to disturb him. He looked at peace while he slept. All the stress that had been etched on his face throughout the time she'd worked for him seemed to have disappeared, leaving nothing but tranquillity in its place. Finding the remote control, Olivia turned off the TV, allowing silence to wash over the room.

As quietly and carefully as she could without waking him, Olivia gently placed the sofa throw over Jake. She didn't want him to wake up cold; that wasn't pleasant for anybody. Then she tiptoed out of the room, pulling the door softly closed behind her, all the time holding her breath, worried that her breathing may wake the sleeping beauty.

In the kitchen, Olivia filled the dishwasher and wiped down the surfaces, preparing to go to bed. She liked everything neat and tidy, everything in its place. It gave her peace of mind. There was nothing worse than waking up to an unclean kitchen first thing in the morning. Humming as she cleared, Olivia missed the sound of the door sliding open, "I have a cleaner to do that. You don't need to clean as well as run around after me," Jake stated gruffly.

"Jeez! You startled me! I thought you were out for the night." Olivia's hand instinctively rose to cover her heart as it thumped inside her ribcage.

"Can't sleep on the floor these days." He shrugged his shoulder in dismissal. Not so long ago, he'd have passed out from whatever he'd taken, and slept where he fell, but not anymore. Being sober left him twitchy. No longer did he enjoy the deep unconscious sleep that being wasted used to grant him. Now he was lucky if he slept for more than a couple of hours a night. He'd turned into a serial napper. He was only ever one creaky floorboard away from being wide-awake. "You should have woken me. The movie was for you. I was supposed to be making up for being an arsehole to you."

"Relax, I enjoyed it. It was a nice change to spend time out of my room on an evening." Olivia ran the cold water tap, filling two glasses. She handed one to Jake and took a sip from the other. Her tongue darted out to wipe any residual moisture from her lips, his eyes heated as she rolled her bottom lip over her teeth.

"Yeah, so I'm heading up now. I'll...see you in the morning." He took his glass of water and made his way up to his room. Flicking the lights off behind her, Olivia keyed in the code on the house alarm and made her way upstairs too.

It had been a long day, and the bubble bath she'd been dreaming about for the last few hours didn't disappoint. With her hair piled up in a loose bun on the top of her head, she slid further down into the luxurious foam, covering her shoulders with the warm, scented bubbles. Only her head and hot pink painted toenails peaked out above the mountain of foam. With her eyes closed, she allowed her head to fall back and rest against the rim of the tub, her mind wandering back over the day's events as she relaxed.

A brief half-cough stirred her from her dream-like state. Olivia opened her eyes to see Jake standing in the open doorway, his arms reached up, gripping the top of the doorframe. Every muscle in his well-toned arms flexed as he held on to the woodwork, exposing a tight band of flesh across his lower abdomen. His eyes skimmed across the bubbly foam before settling on her face. "You said earlier that I'd miss you if you weren't here, if I got Izzie to fire you. Well, I just wanted to let you know that you're right. I've kind of got used to you being here now. You're okay." He sounded almost irritable at the realisation that he'd come to accept her presence in his life. "A little annoying at times, but we can work on that, I suppose."

Olivia took in the full sight of him filling the doorway. Her pulse throbbed low, settling somewhere south of her waist. Great, that was all she needed. Maybe she'd have to figure out a night off and scratch this itch that seemed too persistent all of a sudden. Surely there'd be someone willing to accommodate her neediness.

"Erm, Jake. I'm in the bath. Naked. In my own private bathroom. You know, in case you hadn't noticed!" Thank God for expensive bubbles and the modesty they provided to her bathing experience. As she glanced down at herself, she was pretty sure all the essentials were covered and nothing was being flashed unnecessarily.

"Of course I noticed. What do you think I am,

blind? Unless you have three tits or something else strange going on, it's nothing I haven't seen before, Liv." Jake chuckled, the sound vibrating around the bathroom.

"It's Olivia. And you haven't seen mine before. Nor are you ever likely to. Now get out, Jake!" Raising her arm, Olivia threw the wash mitt across the room at him, missing him by quite a distance as it splatted unceremoniously on the tiled floor in front of him. This only served to make him laugh even louder.

"Liv, you might not want to do that again. Just sayin'." Jake shook his head slowly from side to side and his shoulders rose rhythmically as he tried to stifle the laughter.

"Why? What are you going to do about it if I do, fire me?" she challenged him, her arm poised with shampoo bottle in hand and ready to throw.

"No, of course not. But now I have *totally* seen your tits!" After his startling revelation, Jake turned to make his way back out of her bathroom, chuckling as he went. "Night, Liv."

"Bastard!" She called out after him as she sank low beneath the bubbles again.

CHAPTER
Nine

Turning onto her side, Olivia buried herself deeper into the voluptuous duvet. It felt like no more than minutes ago that she'd slipped beneath the sheets and drifted off to sleep. Although she knew it had to be much longer than that; daylight had started to invade her room, casting shadows on her still closed eyelids. She refused to open her eyes yet. Her morning alarm hadn't even gone off yet; there was no need to rush.

"Morning, sleepy head." The bed dipped beside her and the smell of fresh coffee wafted up her nose. "I don't even know if you like coffee, but I was having one so I brought you one too. Here, it's hot."

The realisation that she was naked beneath the sheets hit her and she clutched the duvet to her chest before turning over to confront him. "Jake! You cannot just let yourself into my room. My room is out of bounds. Do you not understand personal space and boundaries?" With one hand securely clutching the covers, she ran her hand over her face and through her hair, trying to tame the wild tendrils. "I have no clothes on and you're sitting on my bed. Move, Jake!"

He had the decency to at least look a little sheepish as he removed his backside from her bed. "Sorry. I thought I was doing a nice thing. It's only coffee. I didn't crawl under the sheets with you." He placed her coffee cup on the bedside table then walked across the room in the direction of the closet. "I was awake and bored, that's all." He flung the closet doors open and began rifling through the rails.

"What are you doing?" Olivia asked, exasperated as she wriggled up the bed to a sitting position, careful to keep everything under wraps as she did. She glanced at the clock next to her cup. "It's five in the morning! You woke me up at the ass crack of dawn, for what? Because you were bored. Really?" She sipped the liquid nectar he'd brought for her, allowing it to soothe her as she drank.

"Here, shove this on, then you won't be quite so naked." He launched a T-shirt at her from across the room then graciously turned his back while she fidgeted into it. "Done?"

"Yep. It's safe to turn around."

Doing so, he walked back across to the bed and sat right back down next to her, picking up his own drink as he rested his back against the headboard. "I thought we could do an hour in the gym before we head down to rehearsals."

"Are you being serious? When I suggested you start working out again you nearly passed out and had me fired. Is that your plan? To go running to Izzie, telling her I made you work out?" She studied his face, waiting for a response. He was starting to look a lot more like his old self; the stress and worry were beginning to fade from his eyes. Olivia's eyes traced the outline of his strong jaw and settled on his mouth as she willed him to deny it.

"Yeah, that's my plan exactly. I'm going to let you whip my arse on the treadmill then I'm going to tell Iz to fire you." He slurped down another mouthful of coffee. "Do you want to work out with me or not? Hey, this was your idea, after all. There's no catch, just that I may need a bit of motivation, that's all." Working out with Jake was exactly what she wanted to do, but probably not the kind of workout he had in mind right then. What was wrong with her? This had to stop. *Enough already*, she silently berated herself. "Well? Do you want to get sweaty with me or not? Time's slipping away, Liv."

Did she ever.

"Okay, if I must. Give me two minutes to brush my teeth and find my workout gear. I'll see you downstairs." She watched as he stood and walked out of her room. Her eyes lingered a smidgeon too long on his rather gorgeous backside as it swayed seductively as he moved. As the door clicked closed behind him, she let out a sigh. "Get a grip, woman," she told herself as she threw the covers back and climbed out of bed. "It's Jake." She pulled the old T-shirt up and over her head as she walked towards her bathroom.

The bedroom door swung open swiftly and Jake appeared in her room again. "What did you say?" He struggled to keep his eyes on hers as she stood there before him, naked, the balled up T-shirt she'd been wearing clutched to her front as she tried to cover up.

"Have you never heard of knocking?" She screamed at him. "I want a lock fitted on my door, pronto. Do you hear me?"

"Aww, and spoil all the fun? Why do you wanna do that, Liv? It's just me, and I tell you, if I were you, I'd be showing off that hot body any chance I got." At that, he winked suggestively and left her room, leaving her stunned at his comment.

The state of the art gym was housed in the basement. Jake had it fitted out when he first bought the house. It had been an office originally, but he had no need for that. Before he'd decided that alcohol and opiates were much more fun, he'd spent a lot of time down there getting in shape. As he stood before the floor to ceiling mirrored wall, he could see the difference in his body. He'd lost some of the definition in his chest and abs, but with a little hard work he was sure he could get that back. Twisting to the side, he checked out the back view of himself. At least he still looked in half decent shape. It was nothing some bench work wouldn't sort out. Content that he'd assessed the damage accurately, he lowered himself down onto the weight bench, positioning himself, ready to press a few reps out.

"That's all well and good, Jakey boy, but if you don't get rid of the fat first, you're wasting your time." Olivia heckled him from the doorway where she'd been surreptitiously watching him admire his own reflection.

"Are you saying I'm fat?" He grunted as he seated

the weight bar back in its holder above him before rising to a sitting position.

"Nope, I'm just saying you could lose a few pounds, that's all. Then all that effort you're putting into bench pressing will really pay off." Olivia placed her water bottle in the holder on the treadmill, throwing her towel on the floor beside her. She punched in a few numbers and set off at a steady walk as the belt began to turn beneath her feet. Jake watched as she slowly sped up and settled into a comfortable jog. "You need to burn fat then define the muscle. That's how you get the best results." She grinned mischievously across at where he sat. "Can you run?" she quizzed him.

"Of course I can fucking run! Who the hell can't run?"

"You'd be surprised." She sniggered.

"Okay, challenge accepted. I'll match whatever speed and distance you do on there. Just yell when you're done." He laid back down and lifted the weight bar again, huffing out huge breaths as he pushed it away from his chest again and again.

Olivia found it hard to concentrate on her own activity as she listened to him grunting at the other end of the room. Her eyes darted across to where he continued to punish himself, one repetition after another. She could see the sweat running from his forehead as he worked harder and harder. Her own exertion was evident as it ran down the middle of her back. She felt hot and bothered, and it wasn't all down to the exercise. The sight and sound of Jake working up a sweat had her all excited too. Trying to snap out of it, she focused her attention on her own reflection in the mirror in front of her. Picking up her pace, she tried to force images of a naked, glistening Jake from her rather dirty thoughts. Her eyes, however, had other ideas and kept meandering back to watch him as he moved around the room, trying out different equipment as he went.

"Done," she finally stated, thirty minutes later. She slowed the treadmill to a walk and then stopped. Jake appeared by her side and handed her a towel to wipe herself down. "Think you can keep up with me then?"

"Keep up? I'm going to nail it. Watch me." There was nothing like friendly banter in the gym to keep the motivation going. "And you can do that freaky looking-at-me-but-not-looking-at-me thing while I do." He slapped her hard on the arse cheek before taking his position on the treadmill.

He soon became breathless and flushed from the

exertion. "That's eight minutes light jogging you've done. What did you say about '*nailing it*'?" Olivia sniggered around her water bottle as he puffed out his chest and pushed on with the punishing pace. "Little out of shape, are we? Tut-tut, Jakey. Beaten by a girl."

Jake abruptly thumped away at the buttons on the treadmill, forcing it to slow down rapidly and stop. "I just haven't run in a while, and I'd already done a shit ton of weights while you pranced around with your *jogging*." He mopped the sweat from the back of his neck with his towel, wiping his face as he went. Olivia ignored him as she set to work with the hand weights. If he was going to drag her down there at some ungodly hour in the morning then she might as well make the most of it and try to fit in her regular routine. Jake tried his best to ignore the show she was putting on for him, her posture taut and focused as the muscles flexed in her arms as she worked each limb. He moved to stand directly behind her, tucking in so close his chest brushed against her back as he dropped his towel onto the floor at their feet. "Your posture's all wrong. Here, like this." He placed his hands on her hips, manipulating them, forcing her body to contort slightly. "Now pull your shoulders back, nice and straight. That's it. Now repeat the lift." Olivia did as he instructed. Flexing her arms out in front of her, she felt them working harder.

"You feel the difference?" His hands stayed glued to her hips but his eyes were completely focused on hers in the mirror. He was so close to her she could feel his body heat through her clothing, feel his breath float through her hair as he spoke. Goosebumps sprang across her arms like miniature traitors.

"Mmhmm." Was about the only response she could manage.

"Want me to show you some more exercises? We could work on your abs or your arms, whatever..." Jake took a step backwards, creating a little distance. Olivia wasn't the only one who'd sensed the shift in the atmosphere. His fingers made busy undoing and retying the cord on is training shorts while he waited for her to answer. When he risked looking back up at her, she turned around to face him and closed the gap he'd created between them. With a swift and purposeful movement, she lunged forward and kissed him, her lips meeting his head on. Jake stood there in a complete daze, unsure of what to do or what exactly was going on.

As if a lightbulb switched on inside her head, Olivia pulled back sharply, extracting herself from Jake's mouth.

"Oh God, I'm sorry... I'm so sorry, I don't know why I did that. Sorry." Turning on her heel, Olivia dashed from the gym, leaving a floundering Jake open-mouthed and stunned as he stared at her retreating figure.

CHAPTER
Ten

With her face upturned and eyes closed tightly, Olivia allowed the steaming hot water to cascade over her. The embarrassment of assaulting Jake slowly slid away as she ran her hands through her wet hair, pushing the soapy suds away from her face. What the hell had come over her, she had no idea, but she also knew she'd have to face him pretty soon. They were due at the studio in a while and there was no room for awkwardness in his schedule. There was no other way around it, Olivia knew she'd have to pull on her big girl pants and get on with her job. Skulking around was not going to cut it. Neither was avoiding Jake.

"Argh!" She berated herself as she lathered up her sponge and began to scrub away at her body, trying to remove all traces of guilt and shame as she washed.

"Want me to do your back?" Jake's voice was low,

almost a growl as he hovered by the now open glass shower cubicle. Olivia froze as she felt him step in behind her and close the glass door. Feeling his lips on the back of her neck, she closed her eyes as his fingers traced a path down her spine. He groaned against her shoulder as he ran his hands around her torso and up to cup her breasts. His thumbs rolled over her nipples, pulling gently on them, forcing her to thrust them forward and further into his hands.

"Jake, I don't-"

"Sshh. Don't say anything else." Lifting one hand to her chin, he gently tipped her head back against his shoulder as he planted more kisses along the length of her slender neck. "It's okay."

Olivia made an almost guttural sound as he explored her body. His hand came to rest between her legs, fingers sliding through her wet folds and dipping slowly, deliciously inside her, teasing out yet more moans as she arched her body, feeling his hard cock pressed against her back. Turning her face towards him, she allowed him to swallow the sounds he provoked from her as his lips caressed hers. Tongues flicked and danced together as Jake's hands roamed freely along her warm wet skin, holding her tightly against his body.

Allowing her to turn in his arms, Olivia pressed

her breasts against his smooth, wet chest. His hands settled firmly on her arse cheeks, lifting her effortlessly. Her legs came up to wrap around his waist, arms wrapped tightly around his neck as his impressive erection rubbed eagerly at her aching clit.

"I want more. I need more." Her pleading was muffled by Jake's insistent kisses. Untangling limbs and legs from around his waist, Jake stepped backwards and out of the shower, reappearing seconds later with a condom, his eyes never leaving Olivia's as he sheathed his cock. His expression darkened as he advanced on her, lifting her back into his arms, forcing her to wrap her legs around his waist once more. Then, he thrust all the way inside of her, seating his cock as deeply as he could.

"Jesus!" Olivia cried out, causing Jake to still instantly inside her.

"You okay? Did Little Jake hurt you?" Concern etched on his face as he tried to figure out if he should carry on or stop.

"No, you didn't hurt me, and yes, I'm okay, but do not ever refer to your dick as 'Little Jake' for the duration of t...whatever this is."

"It's just sex, Liv, that's all. God, you feel amazing, so much better than I imagined you would. So tight and wet, and so fucking good." Bringing his forehead to rest on hers, Jake took a deep, steadying breath, pulling his senses in line as he did. It already felt like so much more than just sex to him, but he needed to put that thought straight out of his mind.

"Just fuck me, Jake." The slow burning fire Olivia could feel low in her abdomen needed stoking. Right then, Jake was the man to do it.

"With pleasure." His eyes fixed on the bright sparkling ones staring back at him as he pulled his cock out to the very tip and then slammed back inside her again, forcing her to call out in pleasurable pain. And then he did it over and over again, forcing Olivia backwards, allowing the cool tiles to steady them as he pounded into her, pushing her towards orgasm with every thrust. "Tell me you're nearly there, I'm not gonna hold on much longer," Jake inched out of her, giving him enough room to rub the pad of his thumb in languid circles over her swollen clit.

"Faster, harder. Do it harder, please," Olivia begged, her own release so close.

"Trust me, I've got this." His cocky attitude showed through.

"Fuck! Jake! I'm..."

"Coming!" Jake's face contorted in pleasure as he pushed deep inside her, riding out his own orgasm as Olivia pulsated around his cock.

Jake clutched Olivia to him as their breathing returned to normal, holding her steady beneath the still warm water. Droplets ran in rivulets down his back, mixing with sweat as they went. Laying gentle kisses along her shoulder and neck, he murmured as he went. "Let me get rid of the condom. Be back in a second." She watched as his sexy arse exited the shower cubicle, the dimples at the base of his spine appearing to wink at her as he walked. He reappeared a few seconds later, joining her beneath the cascading water. He reached around her, turning up the water temperature as he kissed the tip of her nose. "You surprised me in the gym. I didn't mean to embarrass you." The peppered kisses continued up her neck and along her jaw towards her mouth.

"Don't do that. Don't pick it apart now. It's just sex, you said it." Turning to face him, she ran her tongue along his lips, begging for entry again. He granted her access eagerly, swallowing the air she breathed out.

"So, you're okay with it? The sex?" Hands roamed flesh, rubbing soapy suds into wet skin as he questioned her.

"Jeez, Jake! What do you want me to do, stroke your ego?" Olivia placed a hand on his firm chest, pushing back slightly as she did. Having sex with Jake wasn't the best idea she'd ever had. She could make peace with her actions as long as that was all it was. Just sex. A one-off, never to be repeated hot, sweaty, moment of madness.

Taking her hand in his, he positioned it around his growing erection. "It's not my ego that needs stroking, darlin'." Glancing down, Jake revelled in the beauty of seeing his hard cock encased her in small hand. He hissed as wet, soapy fingers slid up and down his shaft.

"Like this?"

"Just like that." His head rolled backwards, eyes closing in ecstasy. "Feels fucking amazing, but let's get out of here. I want you on the bed." Seconds later, Olivia lay spread-eagled on the bed, with Jake's head between her thighs. Her back arched as another orgasm tore through her, sending a flood of heat to her fingers and toes. Not giving her time to calm, Jake slid his sheathed cock between her wet folds, seating himself balls deep in his new happy place.

With sweat-glistened bodies, they lay in a post-sex haze. Jake's arm coiled languidly around Olivia's shoulders, pulling her into his chest, the weight of her welcome against his body. He felt a peace he hadn't felt in a long time. For once, the itch of his body needing a fix had disappeared and he felt strangely calm as he listened to Olivia breathing steadily.

"I thought you said you rarely had sex in a bed," Olivia teased him. "Or do you make exceptions for the hired help?"

Pushing himself up from the bed, Jake headed towards the doorway. "We should think about heading to the studio. Izzie will be on the phone if I'm late."

Olivia watched the door close behind him, confused and growing irate at his dismissal of her. He'd had his fun and now it was back to arsehole Jake. Well, if that was how he wanted to play it, bring it on. She was more than ready to play that game with him.

Throwing on her clothes and slipping her feet into her comfy boots, she padded down the hallway in search of Jake. She found him perched on the end of his bed with his head in his hands and a cigarette hanging from his lips. As she stood in the doorway, she took a moment to fully appreciate just how gorgeous he was; his dark, slightly overgrown hair had been purposefully messed up, the ink from his intricate tattooed sleeve weaved around his arm and led her eyes up to broad shoulders, shoulders she'd clung to not thirty minutes ago. What the hell had happened? It was sex, he'd said it himself. Nothing more, nothing less. Thousands of people did it every day, but yet there she was feeling like a bomb was about to go off in the pit of her stomach.

"You ready?" she questioned him, breaking the silence as she tried to avoid any further awkwardness.

"Suppose so." Pushing past her, he managed to avoid any eye or body contact as he squeezed through the tiny gap left between her and the doorframe.

"Great," she muttered beneath her breath, before following him downstairs and out to the car.

CHAPTER
Eleven

D-day had arrived. It was seven in the morning and the car had arrived to take them to the airport. The plane was due to leave in just over two hours. She'd checked and double checked their luggage a hundred times since last night, but Olivia still had the feeling she'd left something important out. As the driver attempted to close the boot, she leapt out of her seat again, yelling as she clambered out of the car. "Wait! Is the small brown flight bag in there? I can't remember seeing it."

"For fuck's sake, Olivia. You put it in there. I've seen it, you've seen it, the whole fucking world has seen it. Can we go now?" Jake whined as he grabbed her wrist. "You're making me nervous with all this shit."

"Sorry. I'm just worried I've forgotten something."

"Whatever," Jake grumbled as he lit yet another

cigarette, blowing out the smoke slowly as he exhaled. It had been four days since the sex-in-the-shower scenario, and neither one of them had mentioned it. Nor had they spent any time alone together since. Jake had spent the majority of his time alone in his room or the media room when they weren't at the studio rehearsing. He'd even reverted to eating alone; there'd been no more takeaway banquets with a movie. Olivia had been left feeling a little unsure of just what had happened to make him withdraw again but she wasn't going to be the one to call him out on it either. She needed this job and wasn't about to blow it by alienating Jake even further. That night had been a mistake - he obviously thought so. There wasn't any point in rehashing the details or forcing any discussion with him about it. So they both avoided the subject and each other.

Settling into the journey to the airport, Olivia watched as the scenery sped past the windows, her mind drifting as the buildings and greenery merged into one. Remembering happier times from her childhood, she pictured her father kissing her mother goodbye every morning before he left for work. The look on her mother's face when he walked through the door every night. It was the kind of love she wanted. All encompassing, soul-mate kind of love. Not the tatty, soul-destroying kind she'd experienced up until then. Two ex-boyfriends and one absolute disaster - that was the sum total of her catastrophic love life.

As the car taxied to a stop on the runway, Jake dived out, leaving Olivia to sort out the safe transportation of the luggage from the car to the plane. When satisfied that nothing was left behind, she made her way up the steps to board the plane.

"Hi, you must be Olivia. I'm Kate. I'll be looking after everyone today." The smiley girl held out a hand to shake Olivia's before directing her inside. The interior of the plane was like nothing she'd seen before. Plush cream leather seats like armchairs greeted her, along with neat matching tables. Jake had already taken his seat and fastened his lap belt. He was submerged in colourful conversation with Andy, his new head of security. He didn't even look up when Andy motioned for Olivia to join them in their cosy seating arrangement. He merely grunted as he pulled the hood of his jacket up and plugged his earphones in.

Tightening her lap belt as far as it would go, Olivia looked anxiously around her, checking out her surroundings and any exits. Not that she'd need them, hopefully. Raising her hand, she swiped away the sweat that threatened to fall from her forehead; she couldn't recall signing up for this torture. It was a tin box, when all was said and done, and tin boxes weren't supposed to fly.

"You okay, Olivia?" Andy offered her a water bottle, offering her a gentle, encouraging smile as he spoke.

"Never flown before. I'm not sure I'm going to like it."

"Well it's a short flight today. You'll be fine. We'll be there before you know it. Kate will take good care of us, and the pilot's our regular guy. It's just like taking a bus."

Olivia wasn't so sure but appreciated his sentiments. As the pilot announced over the tannoy for the cabin doors to be locked, and for everyone to be seated, the nerves really kicked in forcing her hands to grip the chair arms until her knuckles turned white. When the engines roared to life, she actually thought she might throw up.

Andy moved forward, holding out a small white paper bag for her. "You've gone a kind of greenish colour. You might need this."

"I'm fine, really," she insisted as the plane taxied down the runway. As the plane reached the correct speed, the nose lifted from the tarmac and began to climb skywards, taking Olivia's stomach with it. "Shit! Gimme the bag!" Leaning forward, she clutched the white paper to her mouth and successfully emptied her breakfast into it.

"Ah, what! Liv, that's fucking disgusting," Jake complained before turning in his seat, trying to put some distance between himself and his ill companion.

"Jake! She can't help being travel sick." Leaving his chair, Andy went in search of Kate and something to clean up Olivia. "There's a bedroom back there. Why don't you go have a lie down? It has its own bathroom too, you know, just in case..." Grateful for the ability to escape further embarrassment, Olivia unbuckled her belt and headed in the direction Andy had indicated. At least she wouldn't have to suffer Jake ignoring her for the next few hours.

As soon as her head it the pillow, she dozed, allowing the hum of the engines to lull her into a dreamlike state. The bed was surprisingly comfortable as she lay coiled in a foetal position, drifting somewhere between sleep and consciousness. The bed dipped beside her, causing her to groan and stir from her stupor.

"Shh, it's just me. Came to check you were okay." Jake settled in behind her, his body lining up directly with hers. "You looked a funny colour. Do you need anything?" His hand swept her long red hair back over her shoulder, exposing her neck and allowing him to see her face. Placing the back of his hand against her forehead, he checked to see if she was too hot or clammy.

Batting his hand away, Olivia shuffled out from beneath his arm and into a sitting position. Pulling her knees towards her chest, she studied his face. "What are you doing in here?"

"Checking on you. I was worried."

"No. No, you were not! You've hardly spoken to me since we had sex, you've not looked at me all day, and you were disgusted when I threw up next to you. Those, Jake, are not the actions of a worried or even slightly concerned friend." Olivia studied her denim-clad knees as she waited for him to answer. When he didn't, she got up from the bed and entered the tiny bathroom. Inspecting her reflection, she decided she looked like shit. Flying did not agree with her. Turning the cold tap on, she allowed the water to flow until it felt icy against her fingers. Only then did she bend forwards and splash her face.

As she patted her face dry, Jake appeared behind her, watching as she studied him through the mirror. "If I said I was sorry, would you believe me?" Her whole body stiffened and her eyes took on a glazed appearance.

"No."

"Well, I am. I just freaked out a bit. I'm not a good option for you. We probably shouldn't have let it get that far, and then there's Iz." He rubbed his hand along the back of his neck; it was his tell, the one thing that gave him away whenever he was stressed out.

"We had sex, Jake. Just sex, and I don't recall Izzie being in the room with us when it happened. Now I don't know about you, but I'm not about to go and give her all the gory details. Hell, I wasn't even planning on dropping it in the conversation!" Turning to face him, she let him see the anger in her face. "You do not get to call all the shots here and you sure as hell don't get to make me feel like a two bit hooker because I bounced on your dick!" With all her worth, Olivia pushed him backwards and out of the doorway. "I like you, probably a lot more than I should considering you're technically my boss, but not enough to let you treat me like shit. It ends now, are we clear?"

Jake took in the full sight of her, his jaw slack in wonderment. His dick twitched, picking that moment to spring to life and try to salute Olivia at full mast from the encasement of his jeans. It had always had a mind of its own, and right then it knew exactly what it wanted. What it wanted was Olivia. "You are so fucking sexy."

"Jake."

"Shut up." One hand caught the back of her neck, pulling her into him, and the other hand encased her waist, refusing to let her wriggle free and forcing her flush against him. He smashed his lips to hers, his tongue seeking entry into her mouth as he nipped at her lips. He felt her body relax against him as she opened for him, allowing him in. The quiet moan she let slip only served to make his dick harder. His lips and tongue travelled down her neck, tasting her as he nipped at her flesh.

Olivia's hands settled on his pert backside, grasping and pulling him in closer. She couldn't get near enough, as his hands tangled in her unruly hair. "What if someone comes in?" she whispered as Jake began unbuttoning her shirt, his hands slipping inside the black lacy cups of her bra.

"Then they'd get an eye full of the most amazing tits I've ever seen." Lowering his head, Jake kissed her now free breasts in turn, his tongue circling the hard pink buds that were her nipples. As he blew gently across the wet tips, Olivia shuddered. Stepping backwards, Jake unbuckled his belt, slipping his jeans and boxers down his legs. "Or they'd see my dick, but that's nothing new." He grinned as his hand encased his engorged cock, stroking up and down the length.

Olivia didn't take her eyes off Jake's hand moving

backwards and forwards, as she quickly disrobed and lay on the already dishevelled bed. "Are you going to screw me or not?"

Retrieving a condom from his wallet, Jake sheathed himself then settled on his knees between her open thighs. His fingers swept along her wet pussy, dipping inside as he did. Large hands purposefully grabbed her thighs and pulled her up to meet his cock. "Ready?" he asked.

He didn't wait for an answer before he slammed deep inside her, forcing her up the bed as he did. "That what you wanted, Liv? My cock buried inside you?"

It was her turn to tell him to shut up now. "Just fuck me, Jake."

CHAPTER
Twelve

*E*xiting the airport in Germany wasn't as easy as the outward journey had been. Jake's security team had their hands full as they shuffled him and Olivia through the madness and out towards the waiting car.

Since leaving the secure bubble of the plane's bedroom, Olivia's cheeks had remained slightly tinged pink. She was absolutely sure that every single person on the flight knew she'd had sex with Jake. He, on the other hand, could not care less what anyone else knew or thought they knew. As they were bustled through the crowded terminal, surrounded by the security team, he'd held out his hand for Olivia, gripping it tightly to ensure she didn't get separated from him, or worse still, mobbed by jealous fans.

As they settled into the back of the car, the driver edged his way out into the moving traffic, avoiding swooning fans as he drove. Jake reached over and grasped Olivia's hand in his, bringing their joined hands to rest on his denim-clad thigh. "You okay?"

Her heart thumped inside her chest. She was positive that both Jake and their driver could hear it pounding away rapidly, and she wasn't sure if it was the excitement and anxiety of running through the masses, or the fact that Jake was still being nice to her after they'd done the dirty deed. Either way, she was more than a little freaked out.

"Liv?" Jake prompted her.

"Wha-... Yeah, yeah. I'm fine." Glancing down at their joined hands made her feel even more uncomfortable. If Izzie found out they'd become colleagues with benefits, she'd surely sack her. "I don't think holding my hand in public is the best idea you've had, though." Olivia inched further towards the window, turning her attention to the scenery as she spoke.

"Fucking hell, Liv. I can't win. I tried to put some distance between us after the first time we had sex, and you hated me for it. Now, when I'm trying to do the right thing and look after you, I'm still the bad guy. What do you want?" He stared at her, waiting for her to answer him.

"Nothing. I don't want anything, Jake. That's the point."

They spent the remainder of the car journey in silence, with their driver and Andy sat in the front, making pleasant, if not stilted, conversation. They'd obviously heard everything. Olivia slumped down in her seat, waiting on the inevitable phone call from Izzie. The call that would prematurely end her new career.

The driver pulled into the underground parking lot of the plush-looking hotel. Andy jumped out to open Jake's door, but Olivia preferred to open her own doors. They followed Andy in silence out of the garage and into the lift as they headed up to check in. The atmosphere was tense as they rode the lift in silence, Andy coughed politely once but Olivia was sure it was to avoid laughing out loud and the damn awful situation.

As the receptionist began assigning rooms and key cards, Jake butted in. "Hi. Can you make sure my assistant, Liv, is in the room next to mine, please?"

"That's not necessary, really," Olivia intervened promptly. "In fact, the floor below will be perfect."

"Actually, I've checked the booking and Ms Mitchell booked the rooms for you. Mr Williams, you and Ms Holmes are to share the executive suite." The tight-lipped receptionist smiled sweetly at Jake and Olivia.

"Cool!"

"No way!"

Jake and Olivia spoke simultaneously. Andy stepped forward, trying to take control of the situation as a queue began to form behind them. "I'm presuming there are two rooms in the suite? If so, they'll take it. Thank you." Holding out his hand, he took the key cards from the confused woman behind the desk. "Lovers' tiff." He winked knowingly at the poor girl. "It'll all blow over, I'm sure."

Throwing his arms around Jake and Olivia, Andy guided them away from the desk and towards the bank of lifts. Olivia merely scowled while Jake continued to look smug. "Listen, I like my job, a lot. I like my balls even more. If Izzie gets wind of this, I know nothing. Whatever you two get up to is none of my business, but keep me out of it. Izzie is fierce. I do not want to be on the receiving end of that. We clear?"

"Man, you worry too much. Izzie is a pussycat." Jake sniggered. "I can charm my way out of anything with her. One look at my baby blues and she's gone."

"Yeah, okay. Whatever you say, Jake. But I'm serious. Keep me out of it."

"Excuse me, but I am still here you know! There is nothing going on between us. You have nothing to worry about. I know what you overheard in the car, but it was a one-off. He will not be getting a repeat performance, I can assure you of that."

The lift doors slid open, allowing the trio to exit onto the top floor corridor. Olivia headed left, looking for their suite. If they had to share, she wanted first pick of the bedrooms.

Andy stopped outside his own door and handed Jake the two remaining key cards. "This is me. Don't be an arse to her, Jake. Play nicely."

Jake looked down at the patterned carpet, appearing to give thought to what he was about to say. "Oh, I intend to play very nicely. I hope the sound-proofing in this place is good!"

Andy head-butted the door in fake exasperation, but could only stifle the laughter that threatened to erupt from his chest.

"We hit the arena in three hours. Do not make me chase you." He patted Jake on the back before opening his own room door. "Be careful, that's all I'm saying. She's a nice girl."

Andy was sure his words had fallen on deaf ears, but he felt happier that he'd voiced his own opinion on the matter. As he closed his room door, he too prayed the soundproofing was up to par. The last thing he needed for the next few nights was to have to listen to those two screwing.

Olivia waited outside the suite doorway for Jake to slide the card into the lock. As soon as the light flashed green, she smacked her hand down on the door handle, diving inside first. "I want first pick," she muttered as she flung open the first door she came across. "Mmm, it's okay but I want to check the other one before I decide."

Jake stood by, amused, as she drifted from one bedroom to the next. They were both exactly the same, with a bathroom in-between, but he'd let her have her moment if it made her happy.

"I'll take this one." She stood in the doorway of the second room she'd entered. "I think it's slightly bigger and it's away from the door." Quite why that mattered to her, Jake didn't know, but it was fine with him. He knew they were both exactly the same size and décor.

"You sure? You don't want one last look at this one first?" he teased her as he flung himself on the bed, exhausted from the travelling. The unsettled feeling had begun again, sending a stinging feeling throughout his veins. His addiction cravings never went away, he just learnt how to manage them better. Right then, he needed to get busy or get wasted. Seeing as one wasn't an option, he pulled out his phone and dialled Andy.

Olivia hovered outside his door, listening in to his conversation like a naughty child spying on her parents. She knew Izzie would be expecting a phone call with a full update very soon, and she wanted to be sure he wasn't checking out any of the local dealers or begging one of the staff to do a run for him. Once she was sure he was behaving, she settled herself on the large plush sofa and finally allowed herself to fully appreciate the luxurious surroundings before she dialled her boss.

Izzie answered on the third ring, "Hey, everything okay? Jake still sober? Please tell me nobody brought alcohol on board."

"He's fine, he's sober, nobody broke the rules." That was if she didn't count the sex they'd had on the plane. "I didn't see a drop of alcohol, and Jake's about to head to the gym with Andy before we go to the arena. So you can relax." She didn't see any alcohol because she'd spent most of the flight in bed with Jake, but the less Izzie knew about that, the better. No point in offing herself just yet.

"Good, great. Okay, well I'll let you get on and I'll speak to you tonight after the gig."

Olivia said her goodbyes and hung up. Jake announced he was off to the gym and left her in peace to soak in a well-deserved tub.

Might as well make the most of this while it lasted.

CHAPTER
Thirteen

The crowd roared in anticipation as the lights in the arena dipped. The floor vibrated as the gathered masses jumped up and down as they cheered and chanted for Jake to appear.

As they stood backstage, Olivia could feel the tension flowing out of him. The atmosphere was fraught with unease as everybody tiptoed around Jake, nobody daring to question whether he was able to handle the next ninety minutes without any mishaps. Jake hadn't spoken a single word since they'd left the hotel. There'd been no conversation on the car journey over. He'd simply shuffled into the back of the car, plugged in his earbuds, and pulled the hood of his jacket high up over his head, allowing the oversized garment to almost shield his face. Olivia had taken that as her cue to leave him alone. The twenty minute journey had seemed to last an age as the silence extended between them. When they'd finally pulled up at the venue, Jake had dived out of the car first, not waiting for her as he had at the airport. Instead he hurried inside, buffered by his security team. Olivia had followed at a trot behind them.

Jake rolled his shoulders as his focus remained on the dimly lit stage, his head lolling from side to side as he stretched his neck while his band warmed up the crowd, teasing them with a slow steady beat while they waited for the main man to appear.

"You ready?" Andy grasped his shoulder, giving it an encouraging squeeze. "They're gagging for you. Go give them what they want."

Jake didn't answer, he just lifted his water bottle to his mouth and glugged down more than half of it, his gaze still fixed on the dark expanse of stage that stretched out before him. The chanting grew louder as the crowd became more impatient by the minute. Handing the water to Andy, he nodded once and moved forward, bouncing on the balls of his feet as he gathered momentum to head out before his fans. He swallowed the nerves as they threatened to rise up and constrict his throat.

Turning, he flashed his boyish grin at Andy. "Just

another day at the office." With that, he jogged out towards centre stage, saluting the crowd as the noise hit a deafening level. "Hello, Germany!"

Olivia watched from the side-lines, mesmerised by his stage presence. The way he played the crowd, pulling them in minute by minute, was captivating. He had them eating out of the palm of his hand. Halfway through his set, Jake made his way into the wings, needing a quick break. As he appeared at her side, she held out a bottle of water for him to take. "What, no alcohol?" The wink he gave her assured her he was joking.

"I don't think so, Jakey-boy. You seem to be doing just fine without it." She handed him a towel. Her eyes danced over his torso and the ridges of his tight abdomen as Jake reached behind him, pulling his sweaty top over his head and off. The work he was putting in was starting to show. Jake held her gaze as he ran the towel over his upper body then reached for the clean shirt she offered him. "I'll let you have a feel later, but only if you're a good girl while I finish up here."

Olivia coughed as she almost choked trying to cover up her ogling tendencies. Snatching up what remained of the bottle of water she'd given him, he headed back out on stage, winding the crowd back up into a frenzied mass.

Thirty minutes later, Jake was back by her side, euphoria seeping from his every pore. The whole team rushed him as he left the stage, grasping at him as they congratulated him on his mini comeback. There'd been man hugs and back slapping as the huddled group bounced up and down on the spot. Olivia had held back slightly, allowing him time to appreciate his achievement. As the team slowly ebbed backwards, he stood tall, his eyes scanning his immediate surroundings, looking for Olivia. When he saw her a few feet away, his whole body visibly relaxed. The grin that spread across his face was pure gold, and she couldn't help but return it. He quickly closed the gap between them and enveloped her in the tightest hug, his arms wrapping around her waist, pulling her in close to his body. "I did it. Sober."

"Yep, you sure did." Her arms came around his back, rubbing her hands up and down as she gazed admiringly up at him. "I'm proud of you."

"Thanks, I'm proud of me too. Now, let's go celebrate with a..."

"Coffee. Juice. Food. All are good options. Come on." Stepping back slightly, she created space to breathe between them, allowing Jake to step past her and head towards the corridor that would lead them to the waiting car. As she fell in step behind him, he stopped and reached out a hand, taking hers in his. Olivia took it without question; it was becoming second nature. Holding Jake's hand felt right. With a gentle tug, he pulled her in step with him as they followed the security team out of the building.

As the external doors opened, they were met with a wall of flash photography and screaming fans. The die-hard ones always hung on until they were certain he'd left. Without missing a beat, Jake signed a few autographs. Olivia tried to slide her hand from his but he merely tightened his grip, and glanced across at her with a puzzled expression. "Where are you going?"

"To the car."

"No, you stay with me. Right here." Jake looked blankly at her, as though he couldn't understand why she'd want to leave his side. Another flash went off in her face and people continued to shout his name, begging for him to turn in their direction for a photo. Jake obliged, but not before he'd pulled Olivia tight into his side, capturing the moment for posterity.

"Who's the girl, Jake?" one man called out. He was obviously paparazzi, wanting his fifteen minutes of fame.

"This is Liv. Say hello, Liv."

Olivia's cheeks flushed crimson as she tucked her chin in and avoided eye contact with both Jake and the photographer wanting a scoop. She elbowed Jake swiftly in the ribs and tried to steer him away. "Ouch! What did I do? Are you tired? Come on, let's go."

Jake allowed Andy to steer them towards the car. He stood to the side protectively as Olivia climbed in the back. He turned to wave at the last few remaining fans before he too climbed in the rear of the car. Andy slapped his hand on the roof, signalling the driver to leave. As the car pulled out onto the autobahn, Jake relaxed, leaning his body into the corner where the door met the seat. Stretching his arm out along the seat back, he signalled for Olivia to move closer. When she didn't, he leant forward, grasped her arm, and pulled. "You're too far away."

He didn't know what it was about her, but she gave him peace. He felt calm and able to deal with anything when she was next to him. The incessant itch he still felt from his addiction was so much easier to cope with when she was within reach. It became almost non-existent when she was in his arms. He knew he would never be completely free of the desire to use or drink again, but for now, he could manage it as long as Olivia was near. As she settled into his side, he breathed deeply, allowing the tranquillity to soothe him further.

"Jake Williams, the cuddler. Who'd have guessed?" Olivia closed her eyes, contented.

"Yep, it'll ruin my street cred, but who cares? You shouldn't be so damn comfy, now shush. I'm trying to nap so I have the energy keep you up all night."

She wasn't about to argue with that.

CHAPTER Fourteen

"Shit. Shit. Shit. Fuckity-shit." Olivia sat at the breakfast table, surrounded by the morning's papers. English and German. Images from last night's gig stared up at her. Every single one of them carried almost identical images. The best ones featured Jake on stage, with the headline stating that his comeback was deemed a success. The worst one was a close up shot of her and Jake backstage, arms wrapped around each other and staring into each other's eyes. That one was in every paper. That was the one she was worried about; that one and the ones that showed her clutching Jake's side as he signed autographs outside the arena. They looked like a loved-up couple. To the untrained eye, anyone would be forgiven for thinking they were in a relationship. Admittedly, they'd gone from a very cool and understated working relationship to jumping each other's bones pretty quickly, but Olivia wasn't stupid. She knew it was nothing more than a pastime for Jake. Once he was safely back in the world where he belonged, Olivia knew she wouldn't hold his interest for long. There were far too many groupies who were too willing to lose their clothes on Jake's dressing room floor.

Olivia dropped her head into her hands and groaned. What had she done? Why had she let her feelings for Jake get in the way of her job? She knew she'd been on a road to nowhere the first time he'd joined her in the shower. That should have been the end of it, but no, she'd allowed it to continue, and look where it had gotten her. Wallowing in her own self-pity, Olivia missed the sound of Jake entering the room.

"Why is Izzie ringing my phone non-stop? I haven't answered yet because I kinda get the feeling she's gonna ring me out over something." Jake took in the sight of Olivia surrounded by newspapers and empty coffee cups, her uneaten breakfast on a plate beside her. "What's going on, Liv?"

"You might want to turn your phone off. She's not going to stop calling until she's sacked me." Olivia lifted her head from the table and shoved the paper towards Jake. "Here. This is why she's calling. I switched mine off, just until I figure out what I'm going to say to her."

Jake read the article and looked over the pictures, studying them closely. "Is this why she's burning a hole in my phone? They're just photos. Don't know what she's getting so fucking wound up about."

"Jake, they make us look like a couple. Especially this one." She shoved the one with them wrapped in each other's arms across the table. "You look like you're about to kiss me! That's what she's pissed off about." Pushing back her chair, Olivia stood and began pacing the room as she chewed on the side of her nail. She was wearing Jake's T-shirt from last night and it barely covered the essentials as she walked back and forth. "I'll pack first and then I'll call her. I can just tell her to email my ticket info and I can leave right away. She can't argue then, can she?" Her eyes flicked to Jake's, questioning him.

Jake closed the distance she'd desperately tried to put between them. Taking her chin in his grasp, he forced her to look at him as he spoke. "You don't need to leave. I'll talk to her. It'll be fine once I've explained. You're not leaving." He tucked her hair behind her ear so he could see more of her face. He wanted to be sure he had her full attention before he continued. "So what if we look like a couple? Is that so bad? I don't care. In fact, I like how we looked together in those pictures. I look relaxed and happy for the first time in a very long time. That's because you were there with me." He picked up his phone and began scrolling through his contacts for Izzie's number. "And just for the record, I *was* about to kiss you. I like kissing you. A lot. I'm not about to let Izzie bully you into-"

Jake was stunned into silence as a tirade of cursing and shouting echoed around the room from his phone. Yep, she was mad, that was for sure. Jake held his phone away from his ear in some attempt to numb the pain she was trying to inflict on him. It was minutes before the line went quiet enough for Jake to speak calmly to her. "Iz, can we just calm down here, please?" Apparently that was not the right thing to say. It only served to force yet another string of angry words from his boss.

"She is not coming to the phone until you calm down. No, I'm not fucking her, as you so eloquently put it, but I might be later, now that you've put the thought in my mind." Jake winked at Olivia as she groaned out loud in dismay. Half running across the room, she tried to wrestle the phone from Jake. Maybe if she spoke to Izzie herself she could put some kind of positive spin on it. Jake turned his back, holding Olivia at bay as he continued to bait the bear on the other end of the phone. "Izzie, listen to me. You know I love you, and up until now you've been the only girl for me, but it's time we moved on. You have Ben, and a baby on the way. I think you need to let me find someone else to show some Jakey-love to. It's only right." He chuckled as Izzie swore down the phone at him. Olivia gave up her fight and slumped down against the wall, holding her head in her hands as she listened to Jake destroy her career further.

"Iz, I'm joking. Listen, Liv is doing a great job. She hasn't overstepped any boundaries, she's kept me focused and sober. Ask Andy. I'm clean. Last night's show was one of the best I've done and that's because Liv was with me. She keeps me grounded somehow. I can't explain it, but anyway, she does. I honestly don't know much about anything, but I can tell you this, if you sack her, I'll walk." Jake slid his free hand inside the waistband of his joggers, his bare back rested against the door frame as he waited for Izzie's response.

Olivia's jaw dropped open, not quite sure she'd heard him correctly. She couldn't let him ruin his career over a few stupid photos. "Give me the phone,

Jake. I'll talk to her." She held out her hand and waited.

"Iz, I'm going to put Liv on, but I meant what I said. She goes, I go." He didn't wait for her response, he merely leant down and kissed Liv gently on the lips. "I'm right here. If she shouts at you, hang up. I mean it." After handing her the phone, Jake moved to the table and poured himself a coffee. There was no way he would leave the room until he knew for sure that Olivia's job was safe. He would not see her suffer because of a few stupid pictures in the press. Trying to appear nonchalant, he flicked through the morning rags. Avoiding the speculation about his love life, he moved straight to the sports section and ran his eyes over the pages. He couldn't concentrate on the words in front of him, he was too busy trying to listen to what his girl was saying.

"So, I still have a job? Yes, I know about the clause in the contract. I did read it. Last night? No, nothing happened last night at the arena." Technically, that was true. Nothing actually happened at the arena and Izzie wasn't asking about what happened when they arrived back at the hotel. So Olivia could say she definitely wasn't lying there. She could tell Izzie was calming down at last. She'd gone from all-out rage to just being annoyed.

Jake watched as the colour returned to Olivia's cheeks. She no longer looked deathly palc and in fear of her life, which in turn made him feel easier. He poured them both a second cup of coffee and carried one across to Olivia. He sat down on the floor next to her as she finished up her call. After sipping at the now not-so-steaming cup, she rested her head on Jake's shoulder. "She said to tell you that she's seriously pissed, but for the moment, I still have a job." For the next few minutes they sat in silence and drank the remaining coffee. Olivia worried about what was going through Jake's mind. "Perhaps I should just start looking for a new job now. It'll make things easier if I go before I'm pushed."

"You won't be pushed. While I'm doing this job, you stay. I'll make sure, promise." As far as he was concerned, there wasn't anything else to think about. "Stop feeling sorry for yourself and get back in my bed. We have hours before I need to leave for the arena and I know just how I want to spend that time." Standing, Jake pulled Olivia to her feet.

As he clutched her to his body, she could feel how much he wanted her. His erection poked at her stomach as he nuzzled her neck, causing her insides to liquefy. All thoughts of the trouble she was in with Izzie melted away as Jake worked his magic, kissing up her neck and along her jaw. When his teeth grazed her bottom lip, she forgot all about the past hour and ran her hands down his back. Tucking them inside the waistband of his joggers, she pushed them to the floor, leaving him fully exposed and his hard cock pressing against her.

CHAPTER
Fifteen

*A*s they lay in Jake's bed, the silence that surrounded them became oppressive, weighing down on Olivia as she contemplated life after Jake. She'd need to find another job eventually; there was no way she could stand by and watch him fall in love with someone else. That would be torture, and no matter how many times she allowed this to happen, she knew it was temporary. Jake was a huge star with an even bigger reputation as a bad-boy ladies' man. He didn't go in for relationships. She'd seen the pictures of him weekly, daily sometimes, with a different girl on his arm. They were always some Hollywood A-lister or renowned high profile model, not your everyday run of the mill type girl. She knew all too well that she was a pastime, his current play-thing. Once he was fully recovered and back in the game properly, Olivia knew she wouldn't hold his attention anymore. She was cool with that, for now. She could protect her heart and just enjoy the ride while it lasted. Lots of people did it.

Maybe if she patched things up with Izzie when they got home there'd be a different job she could do within the company. Work with one of the other acts on the books perhaps, or even just fill in with an admin role. Whatever. She couldn't go home, that was a definite. Making her own way was her only option and she'd succeed no matter what it took. She would not return home a failure.

"Stop it." Warm lips caressed her bare shoulder as Jake moved her long hair backwards, exposing more flesh for him to nibble. His fingertips traced gentle circles on her hip, forcing her skin to tingle.

"Stop what?"

"Overthinking everything. I can hear your brain ticking away with getaway plans and thoughts of what now." His chest pressed against her back, his warmth seeping into her, making her feel safe and secure in the moment. "I'm right, aren't I? You're laid there plotting your next move and what you're going to say to Izzie. Well, just stop it. I can handle Izzie." His mouth continued to trail kisses along her shoulder and up her neck before he nuzzled below her ear. "The only thing you need to be thinking about right now is just how good I'm going to make you feel for the next five minutes,"

Olivia turned in his arms, capturing his mouth in a kiss. "That long. I'm one lucky lady!" she teased him.

Flipping her onto her back swiftly, Jake pinned her arms above her head as he settled between her thighs. His full weight pinned her to the bed. "Wrap your legs around me and I'll show you just how lucky you are." Lowering his head, he ran his lips across her breast and pulled her nipple into his mouth, grazing it with his teeth before sucking roughly at her. Olivia lifted her legs and secured them around his waist, granting him access to her. He slid his cock straight inside her.

"Fuck." He hissed out the word as he stilled, fully seated within her. "You're perfect." He began to roll his hips slowly and purposefully, moving her ever so slightly up the bed with every thrust. His hands released hers and he rested them above her head, protecting her. His mouth recaptured hers, worshiping her with his tongue as his whole body caressed her.

Olivia's hands roamed towards his backside, finger-tips kneading their way into his flesh as his hips drove her further towards release. "I'm near," she breathed out, her whole body on sensory overload. He was everywhere all at once. Inside her, on her, surrounding her; it was all too much. Her insides began to hitch and a heat settled low in her abdomen as the warmth spread throughout her veins.

"That's it, baby. Pull me in. Hold me tight," he whispered against her lips as he continued to rock rhythmically slowly in and out of her.

Her legs and arms tightened around him as her whole body shuddered with release. Jake thrust violently twice more, then stilled as he too tipped over and joined her in orgasmic bliss.

"Hello? Jake?" Andy's voice echoed around the hotel suite, causing Olivia to snuggle deeper under the covers as she tried to drown out the voice. "You in here?" There was a light tap on the door and then it opened and Andy filled the doorframe. "Oh...erm... sorry! I didn't think. I mean I thought you'd be alone or...sorry." He coughed to cover up his embarrassment as Jake's head popped up over the duvet, smiling at his head of security. Olivia, realising she wasn't dreaming and that they had actually been caught in bed together, groaned loudly and disappeared even further under the covers to hide.

Jake's hands shot out from under the covers as he spoke, laughing, "That wasn't me! I'm not touching her. Liv, babe, don't make those noises while we have company. Andy's probably never heard a girl make those kind of noises before." Olivia's arm shot across the bed and punched Jake swiftly in the side.

"Do you want to ring down to reception and have them announce that I'm in your bed? Really, Jake?" Olivia shuffled upwards, clutching the covers to her chest as she did. The last thing she needed was to flash her boobs to Andy. "Hi."

"Hi. Sorry. I really should have just rung but we need to leave." Andy remained in the doorway, his gaze fixed on Olivia's messy just-fucked hair and flushed cheeks as she struggled to string words together in response.

"Yeah, Andy?" Jake sounded annoyed.

"Uh?"

"You can leave now. I'm awake. We're both awake." Jake pulled Olivia into his side protectively, turning her into his body as he did. "We'll see you downstairs in twenty." Andy turned around to leave. "Oh, and if I hear one word of this being discussed outside of these four walls, you're fired. We clear?"

"As fucking crystal, Jake."

When they entered the hotel lobby thirty minutes later, Jake insisted on holding Olivia's hand, despite her protestations about it not being a good idea. He'd simply held steady and firm, entwining her fingers with his as the lift doors slid open. Nobody batted an eyelid. Jake led her through the lobby and out the front entrance, towards the waiting car. Andy was nowhere to be seen. In his place was one of the other team members. Olivia couldn't remember his name and wasn't even sure she'd been introduced to him. The huge guy stood to the side while they slipped into the rear of the car then climbed in the front, signalling for the driver to leave.

"Where's Andy?" Jake was cautious and uptight when he wasn't surrounded by his usual protectors. He'd come to trust Andy, and when someone new showed up, he didn't like it.

The bodyguard glanced at them through the rear view mirror, assessing Jake's mood before he dared to speak. "There was a problem at the arena. He had to go on ahead, but don't worry, it's all sorted out now. He'll be waiting for you when we get there." The guard turned his whole body in his seat so he could look Jake in the eyes before he spoke again. "Do you need anything before you go on tonight?"

If it hadn't been for the fact that Jake's whole body tensed instantly, Olivia may have missed the clue. She was instantly on high alert. Had he been supplying Jake without her knowledge? Surely he wouldn't put his job at risk by doing that? Her eyes flitted between

Jake and the front seat as she tried to quickly assess the situation.

"Like what?" Jake sneered as his grip tightened on Olivia's hand. "Are you offering me what I think you're offering me?" He'd not touched anything in weeks, but he knew with the way she was looking at him they were on the verge of an epic meltdown. He had to make sure he dealt with this properly.

"I meant...forget it. Forget I said anything." Leaning down, he grabbed a water bottle and tossed it back-wards towards Jake. "Here." Jake caught the bottle but continued to glare at the guard until he turned back in his seat, turning his attention to the road before them.

For the rest of the short journey, Jake sat quietly seething as he spun the bottle of water in his free hand, trying to focus his mind as the all too familiar itch rose within him again. The mere mention of being able to get hold of a hit and he was right back to his level ten craving. Olivia sensed his need and lifted their joined hands onto her lap, pulling him nearer as she tried to get his attention. "Talk to me."

"What do you want me to say?"

"I don't know, but sitting there avoiding me isn't working for me."

"I'm clean, for now, although fuck knows how after

his screw up." Jake lifted his leg and kicked the back of the passenger seat. "When we get to the arena, you stay away from me."

The guy in the front seat didn't answer, he only adjusted his position and continued to stare out of the windscreen.

"I'll speak to Andy. Leave it with me. You just concentrate on whatever it is you need to do before you go on." Olivia rubbed her hand up his arm as she spoke.

"No, Liv. I need you to stay with me. If you disappear, I can't promise... I may not be able to still say I'm clean tomorrow. Stay with me." He looked scared. She'd never seen him like this. He'd always been so sure of himself. Even when he'd thrown the glass at her head, he hadn't looked scared, just angry and out of control. Now he seemed vulnerable and small as he shrank down in the seat beside her.

"Okay, I'll be right beside you. I promise." She may not leave his side but she sure as hell was going to make sure the shithead in the front seat never got close to Jake again. Whatever it took, she'd make sure of that. As Jake settled beside her, she pulled out her phone and tapped out a quick text to Andy. If he knew about this she'd have to go above his head and take it straight to Izzie.

CHAPTER Sixteen

"Y ou're fired." Andy flung up the front passenger door of the car, grabbing whatever his name was by the arm, and ejecting him from the vehicle. "Hand over your badge then get your things from the hotel and go back to whichever rock you climbed out from under." With his hand outstretched, Andy scorned his team member.

"I didn't do anything wrong. I only asked if he needed anything."

"Yeah? Well, he doesn't need anything you have to offer him. If Jake needs anything at all, I'll get it, or Olivia will, not you. Now leave." Andy pushed against the large hulk of a man and sent him backwards.

"How am I supposed to get back to the hotel?"

"I don't give a shit how you get back, but you had better not be here or at the hotel when we're done tonight." Andy turned his back and peered down inside the car, assessing the situation and the look on Jake's face. "We all good in here?"

Jake only nodded stiffly as he clutched Olivia's hand harder. He looked pale and drawn.

"Can we just get him inside, please? I don't think dealing with this out here is helping him." She glanced across at Jake, offering him a calming smile as she spoke. "You okay to go inside?"

He didn't answer, just swung the door open and climbed out, leaving Olivia to follow behind him. As he reached the door, Jake halted, waiting for her to catch up. "I'm sorry, babe. I just needed to put some distance between me and that piece of shit. I didn't mean to leave you alone."

"Jake, I'm fine. Let's just get you inside." Olivia reached up on tiptoes and kissed him on the lips. Interlocking his fingers with hers, he pulled her in closer, seeking comfort from her as his nemesis stared back at them. On a scale of one to ten, the ever-present itch under his skin was now at about a five, and settling to a bearable level.

"C'mon." With their hands firmly locked together, Jake led the way inside the arena and through the rabbit warren of corridors that unfolded before them. As they passed roadies and the rest of the security team, nobody batted an eyelid that Jake and Olivia appeared to be joined at the hip. Olivia still felt uncomfortable with the whole PDA, and as such, kept trying to wriggle her hand free from Jake's unforgiving grasp. "What, Liv? Don't you like me touching you?" Jake stopped abruptly halfway along the corridor, almost causing her to lose her balance and stumble into him.

"Of course I do, but I just think while you're working we should keep our relationship... professional. That's all."

"I'm holding your hand. I haven't thrown you on the floor and ripped your clothes off."

"Jake!"

"Yes, I know Andy heard that and probably the rest of the guys hanging around back here heard it too." With a hooked finger he lifted her chin towards him, making sure he had her full attention. "Liv, in case you hadn't noticed, I don't care. They work for me. What goes on tour, stays on tour."

With those few words, Jake managed to destroy any hope she'd built up inside that maybe she could plan a little longer term with him. Once the tour dates were over, they'd be back home and facing a reality she wasn't sure she was ready for. Knowing that whatever this was that appeared to be going on with them would be over in just over a week hit her hard.

"Can you just quit worrying what they all think, please? They don't care, and more importantly, they don't have a hotline to Izzie. So please, just relax and enjoy it for what it is, okay?"

Olivia bobbed her head in an almost invisible nod of confirmation. She was going to have to wrap her heart in steel to protect it. She couldn't stand to have it broken again, and certainly not by Jake. Olivia knew she wouldn't survive that.

"Good." He pushed open the door to his dressing room and held it open for Olivia to enter first. Once they were inside, Jake transformed almost instantaneously into 'Jake the Star.' His persona shifted from his slightly irritated self to the hyped up, ready to get on stage character that became larger than life. As he paced back and forth, Olivia's phone rang. She groaned as Izzie's name flashed across the screen.

"Who is it?"

"Hey, Izzie." Olivia held the phone to her ear and tried not to giggle as Jake made hangman faces at her from across the room. "Oh... well, thanks but that's what you pay me to do; look after Jake." Her face and body relaxed as she continued to talk to Izzie. Catching her attention, he winked at her. The smile on his face was warm and welcome, and Olivia felt it all the way to her toes. As she hung up, he settled on the large comfy sofa beside her. Slinging his arm around her shoulders, he forced her to settle into his side. "She said to say hi. She also was full of praise for how I dealt with the...situation earlier." Taking a tentative glance up at him, she saw the tension flicker across his face again.

"You didn't need to text Andy from the car, but I'm glad you did. I think if that guy had made it all the way in here I'd have caved."

"No, you wouldn't. I wouldn't let you do that to yourself. You've come so far. There is no way I'm about to stand by and watch you wreck all the hard work you've done." Tucking her feet up under her legs, she settled her arm across his stomach as she snuggled in as close as she could. "How long until they call you to stage?"

"Ten minutes, tops. So you'll just have to wait 'til I've finished and got you back to the hotel now."

Right on cue, Andy popped his head around Jake's door. "Everybody decent in here?"

"It might be worth knocking in future, you know, just in case we're not," Jake grumbled.

Chuckling, Andy chucked him a bottle of water which Jake caught deftly with his left hand. "Okay, Jakey boy, you're up. Ready?"

Extracting himself from Olivia, he stood up and

checked his appearance before he answered. "Sure am, and thanks for earlier. You know, for dealing with that fucker." He gripped Andy's shoulder, squeezing it in appreciation.

"Careful, Jake. Someone might see through that hard exterior you proudly show off."

Jake snorted with laughter and cracked open the water bottle Andy had given him. Lifting it to his mouth, he began to chug down the contents greedily. Within seconds he sent the bottle flying across the room, forcing the water from his mouth as he did.

"What the fu-"

"It's fucking alcohol, not water! Where the fuck did you get this from?" Jake raged, his hands gripping at his own hair as he stared down Andy.

Olivia leapt to her feet, scurrying to pick up the half-empty bottle. She lifted it to her nose and sniffed at the contents. "Is that vodka?" Her voice trembled with anger.

Andy held up his hands in submission as he shook his head violently. "I picked it up from that counter there when I walked in here." His finger indicated to the countertop that ran along the side of the room. Beneath it sat a case of bottled water still in its unbroken cellophane wrapper. Andy's eyes flicked between the case of water and the counter top. "Did you get this from that case, Jake? Or did you bring it in here with you?" Andy held his breath as he waited for Jake to calm down enough to answer. As the silence stretched out before them, Andy prompted him again. "Jake?"

"The guy in the car earlier. It's the fucking bottle he gave me." Jake's voice was low and barely audible, his normally boyish features contorted as he realised the guy had got to him. "I was too wound up to drink it when he gave it to me. I put it on there when we came in here."

"Shit!" Andy's face flushed with anger. "Jake...I'm sorry. This is my fault. I should have been in the car with you, not him. I'll ring Izzie."

"No," Olivia interjected. "Jake, she'll sack him. It's not his fault."

"She's right. You didn't give me the drink, he did. If you tell Iz, it's game over for you. I don't want that. You're the only one I can trust these days." Jake waited for Andy to look at him. "I didn't actually drink much of it, just a mouthful...or two. Nobody needs to know about this." Jake's eyes wandered over the bottle Olivia clutched in her hand. Most of it was gone, sprayed over the floor and walls from where he'd spurted it out. His body craved the last remaining liquid. He needed to get control over this damned itch again but he couldn't do that while Olivia stood holding the water bottle like some kind of temptress. "Liv, can you pour that down the sink, please?"

Without hesitation she dashed into the tiny bathroom and quickly emptied the remaining liquid down the sink before bringing the empty bottle back into the room as proof. Holding it aloft, she flicked it from side to side to prove its emptiness. "All gone."

"Good. Let's just forget about it and let me get to the stage." He pushed past them both, making his way out into the corridor that would take him backstage.

"I don't know why, Liv, but I have a bad feeling about this." Beads of sweat rolled down Andy's forehead, and he quickly swiped them away with the back of his hand.

"He'll be fine. Like he said, he barely drank any of it. He's got this." Olivia rubbed her hand up and down Andy's arm, trying to reassure him. If only she felt half as confident about the whole situation as she'd sounded.

CHAPTER
Seventeen

Standing in the shadows, watching him perform, Olivia could see the beads of sweat running down his temples. She wasn't sure if they were from the physical exertion or the amount of willpower it must have taken him to keep his addiction at bay. Studying him more closely, she could see the stress carved across his features. His words were an effort, not flowing from him like they normally did. His whole body was filled with tension that he couldn't seem to shake. Desperation seeped into his voice as he tried to give the audience what they paid for, but Olivia heard his distraction clearly.

Ninety painful minutes later, he was by her side, even if it was only in body. Andy rushed to his side, handing him a towel and a clean shirt. "Great show. There's a couple of media people in the meet and greet room but it-"

"No."

"Jake…" Andy tried to reason with a fraught Jake.

"I don't think tonight's a good time," Olivia interjected. She could see Jake's hackles rising, and the way he kept clenching and unclenching his fists by his sides as he rolled his head slowly from one shoulder to the other surely couldn't be a good thing. "Can you make some excuse? Say he's unwell or tired? I don't know, but just rearrange it. We can organise a Q&A tomorrow morning when he's a bit less… uptight."

Taking the hint, Andy nodded swiftly. "Sure, I'll, ah… deal with it. Why don't we get you two into the car and back to the hotel first?"

"Sounds like a plan. Thanks. Ready, Jake?" Olivia gently placed a hand on his arm as she spoke. She didn't expect him to still feel sweaty.

His eyes fixed on her small hand as she squeezed his forearm softly. He was sure she could feel his pulse racing from the damn fucking reaction his body was still experiencing. One mouthful of alcohol and he felt like the last few weeks had been meaningless. Denying himself his drug of choice, facing his demons, and striving to beat this shit now felt worthless. The hours sat in therapy sessions had all been for nothing. One fucking mouthful had ruined it all.

"Hey, come on," Olivia looked into his eyes, trying

to gauge which Jake she was dealing with. Messed-up-Jake or loved-up-Jake. She sure knew which one she'd prefer. "It won't last. Nothing lasts forever, right?"

Jerking his arm from her grasp, he shook his head, cold eyes focused on the beautiful blue pair staring up at him. "Not now, Liv." Turning his back on her, he set off down the corridor towards his dressing room, leaving Olivia open-mouthed and lost for words. By the time she realised she needed to follow him, he'd ducked inside the room and was already on his way back out, clutching his balled up jacket in his fist. Jake slowed his pace once he recognised she was practically running to keep up with him. As Andy opened the exit door that would take them straight to the waiting car, the cold air rushed in, swirling around the corridor as if it had been sent to make Jake's mood even worse. Tonight was turning out to be so different from the previous one. Last night they'd exited the arena together. Jake's arm had been wrapped around her protectively, keeping her warm and safe from the crowds. Now she felt very much alone as he marched in front of her. Closed off and impenetrable.

Olivia thanked Andy as he shut the door behind her, leaving her alone with Jake and the driver for company, neither of whom were very talkative. Clicking her seatbelt fastened, she settled in for the short ride back to the hotel, her head lolling back onto the headrest as she closed her eyes and blew out a long loud breath.

"You okay?" Jake asked tentatively.

"Not really, no."

"I'm sorry. I... it was a tough night." His faltering voice caused Olivia to open her eyes. Rolling her head to the side, she gazed at him as he stared out of the window.

"It's okay to admit you're finding it hard. I hate it when you shut me out, though. That's worse." She huffed as she folded her arms protectively across her chest, forming an effective barrier between herself and any further emotional harm he cared to try inflict on her. "Or you could just completely ignore me again, that would be awesome," she muttered under her breath. The remaining journey was spent in silence, both of them staring out at the landscape as it whizzed by in a blur of glitzy lights.

Back in the hotel room, the mood didn't lift, both of them going to opposite ends of the suite from the second they stepped through the door. Olivia wasn't about to push the issue any further. It was obvious he needed space to work out his feelings; figuring out how to deal with daily life was proving to be hard on him.

Standing in what was supposed to be her bedroom

doorway, she watched over Jake as he stood on the balcony, overlooking the bright lights of the city below. Wondering what exactly was going through his mind as he chain-smoked, lighting up cigarette after cigarette, she moved closer to the door that would lead her out to him.

"I'm not about to jump, if that's what you're worrying about." His voice was calmer than it had been for hours.

"I wasn't until you mentioned it." Olivia edged out onto the balcony slowly so as not to worry him. "But I am now. I don't think you should be flicking cigarette butts over the balcony. Why don't you come inside? You've been out here ages." Her eyes skimmed across the space. It was almost as elegant as the suite itself, the wicker furniture all co-ordinating with opulent cushions and huge up-lit planters filled with ferns. A few of the cigarette butts had met their fate on the balcony floor, ground up under Jake's foot, no doubt. She made a mental note to have housekeeping clean it up in the morning. It was then that she saw the water bottle. As she bent down to pick it up, Jake tried to kick it out of her reach but he wasn't quick enough.

"Leave it." He stood up squarely as he turned to face her.

"Is this the bottle that had the alcohol in it?" Olivia

turned the label towards her so she could examine it. "Why's it here, Jake?"

"I said leave it." He reached out to grasp the bottle from Olivia. "Give it to me."

Pulling her arm backwards, she refused him. "Why? What use is it to you now? It's empty. If you want water, I'll get you water. Just come inside." The look in his eyes scared her. He was closed off to her but she could feel the anger building and rolling off him.

"I don't want water. I want the fucking bottle! Give it to me!" With his hand outstretched, Jake motioned for her to hand it over.

Dicing with his emotions, she dangled the bottle from her fingers. "No." When he moved towards her, she turned, dashing inside the hotel room, hoping he'd follow her.

"Liv, hand over the fucking bottle. I'm done with your shit." Jake lunged as he tried to grab the empty water bottle.

"My shit? You're the one with the unhealthy obsession with an empty bottle!" It was then it hit her. "Jake, it *was* empty when you picked it up, wasn't it?" She remembered emptying it but she didn't remember checking it was all gone. "Jake?"

The colour drained from his face as his eyes burned holes right through her. "Yes, it was fucking empty! Do you know how I know that? Do you really want me to tell you?" He began pacing in front of her, his fists clenching and unclenching rhythmically as he stomped. She wasn't sure she wanted the truth anymore, more that she wanted a time machine and to be able to go back to that morning before the whole day turned to rat shit. "I know it was fucking empty because I slit it open so I could lick the inside of it clean. There was a couple of drops in the bottom. They wouldn't come out of the lid so I cut it open to get to it." He stopped pacing and stood directly in front of her, his hands grasping his hips tightly. "Happy now? Is that what you wanted to hear? That I caved in?" As she stood there, speechless, Jake pushed past her, heading over to the mini bar. Thankfully Izzie had arranged for it to be alcohol free before they arrived. The worst thing he'd find in there would be chocolate milk or iced coffee. All she could do was look on as he swiped his hand through the contents, forcing them to scatter across the floor before he slammed the fridge door closed in anger. "I need something, anything."

"Jake, I can't..."

"I know, alright!" He screamed into the room. "I fucking know." Neither one of them spoke for what seemed like several minutes, but in reality was merely seconds. If she could have shrunk in size and disappeared into the background, she would have done, but that wasn't an option. Neither was leaving him alone. He was way too vulnerable. Jake took that decision out of her hands and stomped into his bedroom, slamming and locking the door behind him.

When she was happy he wasn't about to reappear to shout at her again, Olivia crept over to the door, pressing her ear against the cool dark wood. She listened intently for any tell-tale signs that he had contraband tucked away. Happy that all she could hear was him strumming his guitar, she set about clearing up the mess he'd created. As she collected bottles off the floor, she had the urge to open one, checking it was water and hadn't been sneakily refilled. Olivia breathed a sigh of relief when nothing but cool still water passed her lips. Thank God for small mercies. When all the remaining bottles had been cleared and placed neatly back in the mini fridge, she grabbed a cushion and her e-reader, settling in for a long night outside his room.

She wasn't sure how long she'd sat outside his bedroom door, but when the sun began to rise, Olivia knew it must have been hours. With her ear pressed to the door one last time, she satisfied herself that he'd finally fallen asleep and allowed herself to move onto the sofa to try and get some rest.

With no bedding to hand, she pulled the only available cover over shoulders. Sleep began to drag her under as the warmth and scent from Jake's jacket cocooned her, making her feel that bit of comfort she needed.

CHAPTER
Eighteen

"Hey." The smell of coffee wafted around her, rousing her from the sleepy depths she'd finally managed to sink into. As her eyes adjusted to the bright light in the room, Jake came into focus, crouched before her, with the cup held aloft as if it were some sacrificial lamb. "Why didn't you come to bed?"

"The small matter of the locked door made that difficult, and you didn't seem to want company last night." She took the coffee from him, sipping cautiously as she peered across the cup at him.

"Yeah, probably not my finest moment." Sitting down next her, Jake lifted her legs across his, and absentmindedly ran a hand up and down her leg as he spoke. "Last night was a total fuck up. I felt screwed. I didn't mean for you to get caught up in the crossfire." His eyes remained fixed on the hand that gently stroked her leg. "Last night was a new low, even for me. As I sat on the balcony dissecting that fucking bottle so I could lick the insides, I prayed you wouldn't come out there and see me, but I still couldn't stop." His hand stilled on her leg. He let his head fall back and rest on the cushion behind him. "I'm a mess. Every damn fucking day I battle against this...need, this itch. I don't think I'll ever be free of it. And now, well, I don't know what happens now."

"Yes you do. You start again. Today is day one. We ring the counsellor and Izzie, and we get you back on track. It was one lapse. One drop of drink. I know there was hardly anything in that bottle. I emptied it out."

"It only takes a drop. Just one single drop, and now I can't say I'm sober anymore." Turning his head towards her, Jake fixed her with his gaze. "It doesn't matter how much I drank, can't you see that? It just matters that I did. Now my whole body is craving more. Even while I sit here with you, what I really want is a drink." Olivia didn't know what to say so she simply sat while he worked through his thoughts. "If Izzie finds out, I'm done. My career will be over. I've already switched my phone off. I'm sure Andy will have told her."

"He hasn't. I spoke to him last night. Told him I'd

deal with it. But I think you need to tell her. She can help you." Andy had been the only person she'd rung last night after Jake locked himself in this room. She wanted to make sure the guard hadn't been allowed back to the arena or the hotel. Protecting Jake was her priority. The overwhelming need she felt to keep him safe from temptation scared her, but she'd go to any length to make certain the poisonous prick didn't get near him again. "Izzie needs to know and it'll be better if it comes from me or you."

"You know, I watched my dad destroy our family with drink," Olivia began. "If I think back over my childhood, for as long as I remember, he was drunk. I never saw him drink anything other than a beer. I never saw him with a cup of coffee or tea, not even a soft drink. It was always a beer." It was her turn to stare distantly into her cup as if it held all the answers. "My mum stopped him going to school stuff with her because she was scared that my teacher would report them to social services or whatever. She loved him that much that even when she couldn't do anything, she still tried to protect him."

"I didn't know. Izzie never told me." Jake appeared visibly shaken by

"Why would she? I didn't tell her. I don't tell anyone. I don't even know why I'm telling you but it just kinda came out. I'm pretty sure she wouldn't have given me a job had she known."

"But it's your dad with the problem, not you. It doesn't affect your ability to do your job. She doesn't need to know about your father."

Olivia let that settle for a few minutes before she spoke again. "But she needs to know about you. You need to tell her about that piece of shit security guard. Jake, what happened last night was not your fault. You didn't go out looking for a drink, your team didn't supply you with it. Some damn idiot found his way in and tried to break you. It's all on him, not you. Izzie can help you make sure that doesn't happen again."

Olivia moved her legs from his lap and perched on the edge of the sofa cushion, coffee cup clutched between her hands. "You're nothing like my father. He never tried to get any help. All he wanted to do was drink himself to death. Which he did quite successfully six months ago. Technically, according to the coroner's report, it was the impact from the truck that killed him, but had he been sober, he could have avoided that accident. He could have saved the poor paramedic from having to try to revive him at the scene. He could have spared my mum the agony of having to identify his body in the mortuary and then having to tell me that he was gone. The drink was too important to him, though. More important than any of those things." Suddenly aware that she was rocking back and forth in place, Olivia took a sip of her now cold coffee, allowing her confession to hang in the air. "You're nothing like him. I see that. I see past the showbiz exterior and see you, but if you're not careful and don't accept the help on offer, well, who knows? But I guarantee you this, I won't be around to watch you hit self-destruct again. I won't watch somebody else kill themselves. Stop it, Jake. Stop it while you still can."

Leaving him sitting on the sofa, Olivia headed into the bathroom. She needed some space after spilling her family secrets, and with the look on Jake's face, so did he. "Why don't you phone Izzie while I take a bath? The sooner you ring her, the easier it'll be."

Olivia leant back against the closed bathroom door, allowing the coolness to calm her. Telling Jake about her father had never been part of the plan; she'd made her peace with it a while ago. Her dad had been an alcoholic; there was no other way to describe it, and no point in dwelling on it. Booze had been his life and the only thing he cared enough about in the end.

Jake stood on the other side of the bathroom door, listening to the water filling up the bath. His hands and forehead rested on the door as he mulled over everything she'd just told him. If he felt like a lowlife before, the feeling was even worse now. Guilt consumed him as he envisaged Olivia growing up with a drunk for a father and a role model. He knew then what he needed to do. He wasn't going to put her through that again.

"Hey, Izzie. How's my girl?" The conversation that followed wasn't nearly as hard as he expected it to be. Izzie had promised not to sack Andy after much persuasion and insistence on Jake's part that it wasn't his fault, nor was it Olivia's. His boss had also organised for a counsellor to be with him before the night was out. When he ended the call, Jake felt a lot less agitated than he had for days.

He had Olivia to thank for that.

Tapping gently on the bathroom door, he waited until she called out for him to enter. Not his usual move, but he somehow felt that she wouldn't appreciate him been a dick anymore. Shedding clothes as he made his way across to the bath, Olivia watched him in silence. "Is there room in there for me?" he asked as she scooted forward, allowing him to settle behind her. Water sploshed over the sides of the tub and spread across the floor. Picking up the sponge, Jake began washing Olivia's shoulders, squeezing soapy bubbles over her skin and watching it cascade down her chest.

"Feeling better?" she asked him as she ran her toe up and down his foot. Her head rested against his shoulder lazily.

"Yes. You were right, Izzie's fine. She's sorting everything out." Dropping the sponge into the bath water, he wrapped his arms tightly around her, hugging her to him as if his life depended on it. "I'm nothing like your dad. I'm sorry you had to go through all that shit with him and then me last night, but I promise, I'm not him. You are important to me. More important than the booze or the next score. Nothing is more important to me than you. None of this matters if you're not here."

"Jake-"

"Let me finish. I've thought a lot about this, and please, just let me finish. I don't want any of this anymore if you're not here with me. All this is just a passing phase, and someday it'll be gone, but I hope when that happens, you're still here with me. That would make me happy. That's what's real. Me and you."

"Nothing lasts forever, Jake. It's unrealistic to expect it to. You'll get past this hurdle and you'll be right back where you belong. Everything you've worked towards is still there waiting for you. It was one small hiccup, that's all. Your sobriety is still within easy reach."

"Will you just listen to me? I've told Izzie we're together, like a couple kind of together. Yes, she struggled a little with that info, but she's fine now. I want you...us... to be more than just a passing fling. I want clingy. I want good morning and good night texts and all the ones in-between, I like knowing that you care. I *love* knowing you care. I want to go on stage and know you're waiting in the wings for me. I want it all." He kissed the top of her head and held on even tighter as he felt her heartbeat increase. "You keep saying that nothing lasts forever, well, you know what, Liv? I want you to be my nothing. Stay with me, forever. I can do this, Liv, but only if you're by my side."

CHAPTER
Nineteen

The fight to pull air into her lungs became intense. His words swam around inside her head, trying to invade her conscious mind. He'd said forever. He'd said he wanted her in his life forever. As she tossed those two phrases around inside her head, her heart clenched a little.

"Say something. I've just told you how I feel and you haven't said a word. Talk to me."

"Please don't mess with me. I've had my heart broken by bigger people than you, Jake, and I swore I'd never let that happen again. You're just scared right now, that's all. I'm that bit of security in your life and you're clinging to it as though everything depends on it. It's not real."

"No. No, it's not that, it's you. I want you and I know you have feelings for me too. I've seen the way look at me, the way we are together. That's all real, I know it is."

Olivia could hear the desperation in his voice as he babbled through his words.

"Okay, let's say we do this... thing. What happens the next time you need a drink or something else, when you beg me to get you something? What if I can't say no to you next time because I'm too invested in us? What then, Jake?" Olivia's mind raced with what ifs as she tried to separate herself from Jake's warm, wet body. Having his chest pressed against her back certainly wasn't helping her to think straight.

"That won't happen again, I've already promised you that." Jake clung even more tightly as she tried to wriggle free. "Will you just quit trying to get away from me? You are not leaving here until we're sorted."

"What is it you actually want, Jake?" Olivia rubbed at her temples, trying to ease the tension that had built there, causing her head to throb slightly.

"You. Look, I know you've been hurt before but I'm not about to do that to you. I'm a lot of things but I'd never hurt you." Jake loosened his grip on Olivia, allowing her to sit forwards slightly. His hands roamed to her shoulders and began to work on the deep knots. He smiled to himself as she let out a small groan of pleasure.

"Why do we have to define it? Why can't we just *be*? You know, like carry on as normal."

"Because I want everyone to know you're mine. I don't want to repeat all my past mistakes with you. We're different. I feel differently about you, about us."

He couldn't explain how she made him feel, but one thing was certain, he needed her. If she hadn't been at the arena last night with him, he knew he'd have sought out that piece of shit guard and insisted he get him more to drink. It would have been a slow descent into depravity again; he knew all too well where that led. But having her with him gave him the strength to walk away, if you didn't count licking the inside of the water bottle.

As his fingers continued to work their magic on the tension in her shoulders, Jake could feel her resistance begin to fade. Bringing his lips to her neck, he gently kissed and nibbled the soft flesh as she allowed his confession to sink in. Olivia moved her head to the side, granting him easier access to her neck and the spot below her ear that drove her crazy. He smiled to himself as she relaxed in his arms.

"Is it just the booze you're missing? Or is it both?"

"Liv, I'm an addict. I'll always be an addict. I crave everything daily. Hourly even." Jake's hands stilled as he spoke, the weight of his words hitting home suddenly. He'd never really be free of his demons. He knew this was a lifelong battle he'd have to face; he just hoped she'd be by his side to help him through it.

"What were you like when you were using?"

"Jeez. A fucking mess. A total fucking idiot most of the time. I'm generally a happy drunk, until I'm not anymore. Then I get angry and nasty. Yeah, not really someone you'd want to spend any time with. I'm sure you've read the press cuttings, seen the pictures of me wasted with some girl or other hanging on me. It wasn't a great time." His brow furrowed deeply as he remembered back to the times he'd thought were the best of this life. He sure as hell didn't want to sink that low again.

"You don't have to tell me, I'd just like to know the real you." Olivia shrugged, brushing off the conversation.

"Talking's supposed to be the great healer, or so the counsellor tells me. I've grown up a bit since leaving rehab, taken a bit of responsibility for what I did. I can see now that it wasn't anybody else's fault. It was all on me. Nobody held me down and forced me to do it." Lifting a wet hand, he ran it through his hair in frustration, pushing back strands from his face as he breathed out a low breath. He shivered slightly, realising the water had started to cool down. "I was trying to put your mind at rest, not open up old wounds and introduce you to my demons. I wanted you to see the better parts of me, not the dark, vile bits that need to be buried away." Reaching out, he pulled Olivia back towards his chest. Holding her against him again, he slid them both a little lower into the water.

"Your demons don't scare me, Jake."

"Well, they should. They scare the ever living shit out of me."

Olivia startled at his words. She'd never imagined he was scared. He came across as confident and self-assured. In the few weeks she'd worked for him, she'd never once presumed his actions were those of a frightened man. Olivia lifted herself out of the water and turned to face Jake. Kneeling between his thighs and with her hands resting on his chest, she spoke directly to him. "What exactly are you scared of?"

"Everything. Losing the battle, sinking back into the old routine and not being able to see the exit signs again. I'm scared you'll see the real me and walk out." Grasping her around the waist, Jake lifted her up onto his lap, pulling her back into his chest. "You make me want to be a better man. To be the best that I can be, for you."

As Olivia lay with her head tucked beneath his

chin, she realised that despite last night's hiccup, she was where she wanted to be.

With Jake.

If that meant risking her heart, then so be it.

"Okay." She sighed.

"Okay? Okay what?" Jake pushed her forwards slightly so he could see her face. He studied her eyes, looking for any hint of confusion or doubt. He needed clarification.

"I'm willing to give this... *us* a go." Lifting her eyes, she fixed him with a determined stare. "But if you relapse, or cave in, or just decide that drinking or drugs is a good idea again, I'm out. Completely. Done. You have to stay clean and sober while we're together. The second you're neither of those things, I'll leave."

"Are you serious?"

"About the drink and drugs? Absolutely."

"I meant about me. Are you serious about me?" Jake's mouth curved up slightly as he watched her intently.

"I have a lot of doubts, and I can't promise anything, but yes, I'm serious. There is one more condition, though." She tried her best to look sternly at him, even though the look on his face made him appear like a child on Christmas morning who just unwrapped the most amazing present. "We take it slowly. No big announcements to the guys or anything crazy like that. We ease into this gently, okay?"

"Anything you say, baby. Any way you want." Jake kissed her softly, his lips travelling over hers gently, caressing her mouth with soft tender touches as he pulled her into him. His hands roamed down her bare back. Settling on her bottom, he pulled her up against his erection and allowed her to feel just how happy she'd made him.

Taking the hint, Olivia lifted on her knees and sank down on him. His eyes closed in ecstasy when she began to slowly ride him. "How long until we have to be at the sound check?"

"Don't worry about it. They can't start without me."

CHAPTER
Twenty

Sound checks were the best part of the night as far as Olivia was concerned. She got to sit in the arena and experience the full effect as the crowd would later on in the evening. Listening to Jake and the guys make last minute adjustments to their instruments as they ran through the set list was like watching pure genius at work. She'd taken up residence on the front row of seats to work through a few emails as Jake prepared for the evening, that way she could keep an eye on him and give him the reassurance he needed all at the same time.

Engrossed in an email she'd just received from Izzie about Alex and Ben flying in later that day, Olivia hadn't noticed how quiet the arena had become. More and more as the days passed, she'd taken on more responsibility regarding Jake's life in general. She was more than just his babysitter now. With Izzie's heavily pregnant state and his hectic schedule, it made sense for their boss to pass over more mundane tasks to her. She was enjoying the freedom it afforded her, allowing her to feel less need to check in with Izzie over every minor detail. As she pondered over the way her role had evolved, the sound of Jake's guitar drifted out over the arena. Looking up, she realised he was alone up there, the others gone off to eat or nap, no doubt, before the gig. Jake appeared lost in his own world as he strummed out chords to a song that sounded vaguely familiar to her. It wasn't one of his, she was sure of that, but she just couldn't make out the words as he sang quietly, almost to himself.

She was too lost in trying to make out the song that she missed Andy taking up the seat beside her. "He doesn't realise how good he is, does he?"

Olivia startled slightly when he spoke, causing her tablet to almost clatter to the floor. "I don't think he does, no. Who's picking Alex and Ben up from the airport? Are you going?"

"Ben's arranged a driver. I'll be here with Jake all night. Wherever he goes, I go. After what happened yesterday, I'm not taking any more chances. How's he been today?" Andy turned in his seat to address her.

"Okay, I think. Better than I expected, anyway.

Thanks for letting him talk to Izzie first. I know you were worried how that would go."

"Yeah, I still am. She read me the riot act and I'm officially on a last warning, but I don't blame her. It's my job to keep him away from all that shit. I let them both down."

Olivia couldn't see a reasonable argument in that but it wasn't her job to school Andy in his. He held the upper hand here; he had seniority over her. She was merely the hired help. Andy had been a part of Izzie's team for a long time. He'd be fine once they got back home and he could talk to her face to face.

"Is that why she's sending the big guns over?"

"You mean Ben and Alex? I dunno, but probably. I think Jake wanted to have them appear with him during the tour originally but it was never finalised, so who knows." They both turned their attention back to Jake, who seemed to be oblivious to them still as he switched from singing his own songs to trying his hand at a few covers he loved as he tinkered with his favourite guitar.

"Are you sure it's a good idea? You and him, I mean?" Andy questioned her.

"No, not at all." Olivia puffed out a breath. "I don't know. I don't really know what's going on, to be honest. One minute he's all loved up and then the next... well, the next he's just not."

"Look, it's none of my business, but I like you, and I don't want to see you or Jake get hurt. He's put a lot of work in these last few weeks. He's tried really hard to get himself together again." Andy glanced sideways at Olivia, his hands fidgeting in his lap as he worked out how not to offend her. "I don't think he's relationship ready just yet. I'm not sure he's able to handle the pressure of having to look after someone else as well as himself right now. It needs to be all about Jake, keeping him away from the temptations in life, you know?"

"I don't need looking after. I can take care of myself. Do you really believe I'd do anything to hurt him? In case you hadn't noticed, I actually quite like him. In fact I like him a lot." The anger seeped through her as Andy tried to justify his words.

"No, I don't think you'd hurt him on purpose. I'm worried about you too. You're both running around blinkered to exactly what's going on here." The sweat beaded on his forehead as he looked for a way to make things better. "All I'm saying is that if you're in this for a bit of fun, that's fine. Just make sure Jake knows that's all it is. Don't break him again."

Olivia stood, shaking with anger. "I know he's vulnerable, Andy. I get it. But what you don't seem to get is that he's a grown up. He's also a recovering addict. If you don't let him work through it, how the hell is he supposed to get better?" Olivia pushed past Andy, making her way to the end of the row of seats, leaving Andy to flounder after her.

"Baby, what's wrong?" Jake made his way down the steps at the side of the stage toward Olivia, concern etched on his face as he reached a hand out to grasp hers.

"It's my fault. I think I said the wrong thing, or at least the right thing came out all wrong." Andy stumbled through an apology of sorts.

"Liv?" Placing a finger under her chin, Jake lifted her face to his. "What did he do?"

"Nothing. It's okay. I'm fine." She pulled her chin from his grasp and tried to move away, heading back towards the rear of the arena.

"No you're not. Don't lie to me. Talk to me or I'll just make Andy talk."

Olivia traded glances with Andy. They both knew Jake was a loose cannon even at the best of times. If he thought Andy had upset her, there'd be hell to pay.

"I was just having a moan about all the crap I have to put up with in this job and Andy pointed out how well I get paid for putting up with that crap. I didn't like that he stated the obvious, but he's right. I have a job to do." She stared at Andy as he squirmed on the spot beneath Jake's scrutinising stare.

"That doesn't make any sense. I call bullshit on that but I can see you two have some kind of pact going on, so I'll drop it." Wrapping his arm tightly around Olivia, Jake pulled her protectively into his side before turning his full attention to Andy. "I don't know what's going on here but I'm guessing it's done with?"

Andy simply nodded as he walked away from both of them, leaving them alone in the vast, seated arena. When he was sure they were alone again, Jake pulled her into his chest, hugging her tightly. Despite the difference in height, they fit together nicely, her head resting snugly beneath his chin as her arms wrapped tightly around his waist. Jake's hand settled underneath her long hair, his fingertips stroking gently at the base of her neck as he waited for her to relax.

"Did he really upset you?"

"No, not really. I just overreacted, that's all. Don't worry about it." Jake's free hand started to move slowly up and down her spine, trying to ease away the tension for her while pulling her in even closer to his body.

"I'll talk to him if you want me to."

"You'd do that for me?"

"Of course I would. Just say the word."

Sighing deeply, Olivia pulled back slightly so she

could look up at him and see those gorgeous eyes staring back at her. "Honestly, I'm okay. No need for your knight in shining armour act. Well, not today, anyway."

Jake snickered "I'm no knight in any sort of armour. More your wolf in sheep's clothing kinda guy."

"Yeah, but you're my wolf, right?"

"All yours, baby." He kissed the tip of her nose. "But now I have to get back to this thing they call work. You be okay for a while longer? You can sit up here with me, if you like."

"I'd like that." Taking his hand, Olivia followed Jake back up the stairs that led to the stage where she sat for the next hour, watching him tweak the evening's show to perfection.

CHAPTER
Twenty-One

"*H*ey, hey, hey! Look who it is?" Pulling Jake into a man hug, Ben back-slapped him hard. "How's it going? Izzie's worried about you and that's not good for a pregnant lady." Alex followed suit, gripping Jake's shoulder in greeting.

"Al, good to see you! Are Grace and Harley here too?" Jake peered over Alex's shoulder, looking for the girls.

"Nah, they're keeping Izzie happy at the beach house for a few days. All girls together. I think Harley will keep them both busy, though. She's kind of a tear-away right now. A real daddy's girl." The pride shone in Alex's eyes as he spoke about his baby girl.

"Shame. Would have been great to see them both. I want Liv to meet Grace."

"Yeah, I've heard a lot about you from Iz. Nice to

meet you." Alex held out a hand for Liv to shake, politely ignoring the fact that she was blushing crimson from her neck upwards. Olivia stumbled through a polite 'hello' with her high school idol and quickly turned her attention to Jake again.

Ben went for a more direct option and planted a kiss on her still hot cheeks. "How you holding up? He's not giving you too much trouble, is he?"

Olivia shook her head. She may have been more used to being around Ben, what with him being married to her boss, but she was still a little star struck whenever he was occupying the same space as she was. "He's behaving himself, just." She gave Jake a sharp dig in the ribs as he slung his arm around her shoulders. He was making a point about their status, she knew that, but this probably wasn't the time or the place. Alex noticed immediately how uncomfortable she looked and merely smirked at Jake as he held up his hand to high five him.

"Okay, I think it's safe to leave you in the care of these two for a short while. I have to catch up with Andy and go over a few details for tonight." She patted Jake squarely on the stomach as she tried to disentangle herself from the arm he had wrapped around her. "You need anything before I go?"

"Nah, I'm good. We're just gonna go over a few of

the tracks for tonight, right guys?" Ben and Alex nodded in agreement as Olivia made to leave. "Erm, I think you forgot something vital here." Jake stood with his arms crossed over his chest, one eyebrow cocked in her direction.

"What?" Olivia patted down her pockets, checking for her phone and access passes. Nope, they were all intact. She gave him a quizzical look.

Jake patted his cheek with his fingertips. "My kiss."

Olivia's cheeks flushed. Thank God for the dimmed lighting in these places. "Jake, stop it! I'm only going back there to meet with Andy." Her eyes lowered as Ben and Alex watched the exchange with amusement. When she realised Jake wasn't going to let her go without, she stepped forward and pecked his cheek lightly. "Happy now?"

"Not really, no, but it'll do for now." Jake smiled, his eyes shining brightly as she shook her head in disbelief at him before backing up and leaving him with Ben and Alex.

Ben let out a low whistle. "You sure are punching way above your weight there, man!"

Jake laughed loudly at the remark. "Sure am. So, which track do you want to go over first?"

Andy sat waiting in one of the rooms at the rear of

the arena. When Olivia walked through the door, her eyes met with the assortment of sandwiches and nibbles that awaited her on the table. Her stomach growled in anticipation. "Sorry, I'm starving," she muttered as she slid into the chair opposite the large security guard.

"Don't apologise. Dig in. Is Jake with Ben?"

"Nah, I left him talking to some shady-looking guy who said he had some good stuff Jake might be interested in." She avoided his gaze as she picked at a couple of the sandwiches, checking their fillings. Andy coughed wildly as he tried not to choke on whatever he'd just tried to swallow. "Joking! Of course he's with Ben. What do you think I am, some kind of amateur?"

"Look, I've been around the three of them for a long time. Some of the stories I could tell you about them are pretty insane, that's all. I wouldn't put it past Jake to try anything to get his own way."

"You mean you were around for all the sleazy stuff with Uni-Fi too? The groupies with all their antics?"

"The whole damn lot."

"Right, you have to tell me. Spill the gossip." Olivia's eyes lit up with glee, the thought of hearing some of the stories she'd read in the newspapers was too much to miss out on. She rubbed her hands together excitedly as she moved forward, resting her elbows on the table, ready to hear it all.

"I could tell you, but then I'd have to kill you. I'm sworn to secrecy, sorry." Andy laughed at the disgruntled expression on her face. "Just take it that all the stuff you read about them is mostly true, and generally you only got the watered down version. Those boys had revolving doors on their hotel rooms; one in, one out in those days. Jake's been just as bad but he has different demons these days."

Olivia thought about that for a moment. He sure did have demons to fight, but he seemed to be coping better. He'd not lapsed since water-bottle-gate. He seemed brighter, more cheerful, and he hadn't complained about any cravings since then. Perhaps he'd turned a corner. She snorted to herself at that thought. She of all people knew that addicts didn't turn corners. Well, hardly ever, anyway. But he did seem to have a handle on it.

"Do you think he'll be okay? I mean, do you think he'll end up back where he was a few months ago, drinking and taking all that shit again?" Olivia knew nobody had the answer to that question but she felt better for asking it out loud.

"Who knows? He's a law unto himself. Sometimes he self-medicates, sometimes he doesn't. With Jake, I think it all depends on which way the wind blows. Simple as that." Andy offered her a reassuring smile. He knew what she was asking but he couldn't give her any guarantees; it was best not to build any hopes in this job. "Now, shall we get on with what we're supposed to be talking about?"

CHAPTER
Twenty-Two

oday was a day off. One whole day to do as she pleased. Jake had completed three nights of his rescheduled tour, he'd do one more show the following night in Munich, then they flew back to London the next day. After that, Jake had some down time before he'd go back to the studio and begin working on his next album. Olivia couldn't wait to get back home. She'd come to think of her room in Jake's house as her home, and she missed it. Damn, she even missed Izzie.

She lazily stretched out in the bed she'd continued to share with Jake, listening to the shower run. He must have sneaked out of bed to avoid waking her. Normally it was the other way round, with her sneaking around while he snoozed late into the day. Her phone beeped on the bedside table, grabbing her attention. She tapped on the screen to open up a message from Ben.

Morning. His lordship isn't answering so I'm just letting you know we all have dinner reservations at 7.30 tonight. See you then.

She was quickly typing out a response, letting Ben know she'd pass on the message, when Jake appeared from the bathroom. "Morning, gorgeous. Who's that?" he asked, indicating to her phone.

"Ben. He's made reservations for you all tonight at 7.30. He's probably texted you." She smiled and turned her phone to show him the message. Jake nodded before picking up his own to check the details.

"So, what do you want to do today? We have the whole day to ourselves." He climbed onto the bed beside Olivia, leaning over to plant a kiss firmly on her mouth.

She pushed him away gently. "I haven't brushed my teeth!"

"I don't care, come here." He pinned her down with another more forceful kiss. "As much as I'd love to spend the day in bed with you, I think we need to get out for a bit. Do something a bit coupley. Andy's got a driver waiting for us so you'd better get your lazy arse out of bed." The playful slap he gave her backside resonated around the room.

"Coupley! Really? Like what?"

"We're going sight-seeing. I've been here three times and all I've ever seen is the inside of hotels and arenas. Goes with the job, I suppose. We'll do the tourist thing, then stop off for lunch somewhere nice." He dragged the duvet from the bed, exposing her naked flesh to him. "Or, on second thoughts, I could cancel the driver and we could just fuck all day. Damn, woman." Hot, needy eyes roamed her body from top to toe, taking in every inch of her.

Olivia leapt from the bed like a ninja. "No! I want to be a tourist. I'm up." Running past him, she dived into bathroom and under the hot shower, ignoring his cries of dismay.

"You have five minutes, then I'm calling Andy to cancel the driver. Clock's ticking, babe!" he called to her through the steamed up bathroom.

With seconds to spare, Olivia stood, dressed and ready by the hotel room door, waiting for Jake to check he had everything. When he finally appeared, he was barely recognisable, his face covered with huge sunglasses and a baseball cap pulled down over his eyes. If it wasn't for his tattoos, he'd have been able to blend into any crowd.

"Ready?" Olivia asked coolly as she checked her watch.

"Smartass!"

Pulling open the door, he allowed her to exit first and followed her down the corridor to the bank of lifts that would take them straight to the underground garage and their waiting car. "Where are we going?" Olivia asked again. She didn't really care. Having the day off to spend with Jake was more than enough for her, but curiosity got the better of her.

"Andy suggested we head to the main plaza. We should be able to walk around there. Apparently there's some nice restaurants for lunch too, but we can look at the old buildings if you like that sort of thing?"

"Are there shops too?"

Jake nodded. "Yeah I think so, but I don't know which ones. Just so you know…" The lift doors opened, allowing them to step inside. Jake looked sheepishly at her out of the corner of his eye before he continued. "Andy's arranged for Gav to come with us. I kind of have to have someone there, you know, for safety. Sorry."

"Don't apologise. I'm just glad it won't be down to me to fight off the hordes of screaming fans. I'm not sure I'm up for that today." Olivia smiled reassuringly at him. "I'd have been worried if you didn't have security with you. Besides, Gav's funny. It'll be fun." His shoulders relaxed visibly; he'd obviously been worried about breaking it to her that it wouldn't be just the two of them. "Jake, I understand. Your job isn't your everyday one. You attract attention wherever you go. Security is a necessary part of your life. Don't stress about it."

When they reached the garage, Gavin was leaning against the limo, waiting for them. "Morning, boss." He greeted Jake cheerfully as he opened the door to allow Jake and Olivia to climb inside. "Don't worry, Olivia. You'll hardly notice I'm tagging along on your date." The bodyguard winked as Olivia dipped inside next to Jake.

The main plaza was bustling with tourists when they arrived. True to his word, Gavin stayed in the background, allowing the loved-up pair to stroll around, wrapped up in each other and the surroundings. Jake relished being invisible for once. Not one person seemed to recognise him, or if they did, they left him alone to enjoy the tranquillity. The ever-present cravings were at an all-time low and he was happy. Strolling from street to street with his arm casually strung around Olivia's shoulders gave him the kind of peace he strived for.

"I miss this," Jake muttered whilst planting a kiss in Olivia's hair as she looked longingly at the bling on show in the shop windows. "I forget what it's like to just blend in sometimes. Nobody here cares who I am or that I'm here. They're all too busy enjoying themselves. It's nice."

"So full of your own self-importance, that's your problem!" Olivia teased as she fought to keep the laughter from her voice. "Just remind me, who exactly are you?"

"Very funny. C'mon, I'm starving. Let's go find somewhere for lunch." He pulled her away from the shop windows and towards a side street that housed a few restaurants.

Sitting at a table outside a bistro, the three of them were enjoying a relaxing lunch when Jake's phone chimed with a familiar ringtone. "Hey, Iz. How's my girl?"

Jake's face went from relaxed and happy to stony and filled with anger in an instant. "You're sure? Can I take legal action?" That had Olivia's attention immediately. Picking up her phone, she checked for any missed messages from Izzie but came up blank. Whatever it was it must have been big for her to go straight to Jake with it. Olivia and Gavin exchanged worried looks as they waited for Jake to end the call.

When he did, it took him a minute to gather his thoughts before he spoke. "It was Graham." When neither of them responded, but sat there looking lost he continued. "The guy with the water bottle full of booze? Graham sent him. He somehow managed to get the wanker inside the team without Andy realising and paid him to supply me with booze." Jake stared blankly through Olivia while he let the words settle. "He's also trying to sue Iz for unfair dismissal. He doesn't think he should have lost his job because I couldn't stay sober." Lifting his hand, Jake beckoned for the waiter, asking for the bill. "Gav, can you get the car? I've had enough."

"But he can't. Surely-" Olivia didn't have a clue what she wanted to say. Everything swimming around in her head seemed like the wrong thing to say.

"Don't, Liv. Not now. I just want to go." Pushing to his feet, the chair scraped backwards with a screech. Jake scribbled his name on the receipt then held out his hand for Olivia to follow. She didn't hesitate, nor did she say anything else.

Wallowing was something, she'd come to realise, that Jake needed to do occasionally.

CHAPTER
Twenty-Three

ollowing the Maître d through the restaurant, Olivia felt self-conscious. The white linen tablecloths almost glistened in the dimly lit dining room. Crystal and silverware shimmered as the clientele feasted on fine foods and drink. She'd begged Jake to leave her at the hotel but he'd insisted she join him or he wasn't going either. So there she was, about to spend the evening with Ben, Alex, and Jake. Like some kind of spare wheel, no doubt. Alex stood in greeting as they reached their table, shaking Jake's hand before kissing Olivia's cheeks.

"You look lovely, Liv." Ben smiled as Olivia fidgeted with the hem on her dress, pulling it down towards her knees. It had been a panic buy in the hotel lobby boutique when she realised Jake wasn't about to let her get out of the evening's festivities. Her credit card had taken a hit which was worrying but necessary. No way would her jeans and Converse have cut it in those surroundings.

"Thank you. You're not so bad yourself." She managed to muster up an almost funny retort before picking up the menu and browsing through the options. Thank goodness for business expense accounts; this place was out of her league. After settling on a house salad and a chicken dish, Olivia sipped on sparkling water while the boys talked shop.

"Jake? I thought it was you!" Turning her head, Olivia was met by a pair of long slender legs attached to an even longer slender body. A body that belonged to Stacey Freeman, Hollywood A-lister, and one of Jake's past conquests. Olivia's eyes travelled the full length of the actress, from the Louboutins to the perfectly made up, flawless face. She was gorgeous. Without a strand of hair out of place and primped to within an inch of perfection, she blew all other females in the room out of the water without even trying.

Jake stood, leaning in to kiss the actress' cheek awkwardly. "Hey, looking good, Stace." He shifted uncomfortably from one foot to the other as he introduced her to the others around the table. "You know Ben and Alex." Both of them stood to exchange air kisses with the delectable Stacey as Olivia waited. "And this is my girlfriend, Liv. Liv, Stacey Freeman."

He gestured clumsily between the two women vaguely as Stacey brushed over the introduction, leaving Olivia feeling even more uncomfortable. Images of Stacey and Jake together having hot sweaty monkey sex flooded Olivia's mind. Pushing them away proved difficult given that the actress had some kind of affliction that meant she had to touch Jake at every opportunity. She'd stood at the table for roughly three minutes, and in that time she'd touched him no less than thirty times. Olivia knew that for sure; she'd counted every single one of them. Olivia calmly berated herself for the feelings of jealously that were slowly taking over her whole body. After all, she had no claim over him. The hook ups he'd had previously were none of her business. She had no right to make claims on him or his past. And most probably not his future either. This was exactly the kind of thing she'd wanted to avoid. Falling for someone like Jake meant that all his ex fuck buddies were going to be famous and beautiful. Something Olivia knew she could never compete with, not in a million years.

Olivia's eyes lowered, resting on where Stacey's fingers caressed Jake's calloused fingertips. He was doing nothing to stop the tiny touches she kept affording him, and his expression gave away the fact that he was actually enjoying the attention. The anger rose again in her chest, forcing her to excuse herself from the table, leaving them to fondle each other as she headed to the bathroom to allow herself time to cool off.

After taking care of business, Olivia stood at the wash basins, taking in her reflection. Just quite what Jake saw in her, she didn't know. There was nothing special about the Plain Jane staring back at her, in fact, it was quite an ordinary girl-next-door kind of thing she had going on. The bathroom door swung open, and in breezed the stunning Stacey, flicking her hair and swinging her hips with pure attitude. Great, that was just what she needed. Olivia finished up washing her hands before turning to leave the restroom.

"I wouldn't get too comfortable in Jake's bed if I were you. It's obvious to anyone with eyes that he wants me back," Stacey sidestepped Olivia to admire herself in the mirror. Pouting at her own reflection with the universally stupid duckface pose, Stacey primped her perfect features. "Someone like you couldn't hold his interest for long. Believe me, he'll be back in my bed before you know it." Taking one final look at her reflection, Stacey smiled sweetly at Olivia through the mirror. "No hard feelings, darling." The words dripped saccharine sweet from her cherry lips before she turned and exited the bathroom.

In frustration, Olivia let out a disgruntled growl, aiming it blindly at the door Stacey had just exited through. She didn't need anyone else to point out the she wasn't good enough for Jake; she knew that already. But she was damn sure she wasn't going down without a fight. The bathroom door flew open again but this time Jake raced in. "Babe?" His arms outreached to capture Olivia's hands in his. "Are you okay? I was waiting outside for you and heard you kind of scream... I think? What happened? Are you hurt?" His eyes ran over her body, looking for any damage.

"No. Well, not unless you call verbal humiliation being hurt." Olivia shook her hands free of his grasp. "I'm fine. Lady Stacey of the Manor just warned me off you, that's all." Taking a long look at Jake, Olivia watched his reaction for any signs that he wanted Stacey. "Why were you waiting outside the ladies?"

"I...ah...I saw that Stacey headed over this way after you and... well, I just know what she's capable of. I was worried about you. Is it a crime to worry about my girlfriend?" Jake looked defensive as he spoke.

"Is that what I am now? Because Stacey thinks you want her, not me." Olivia crossed her arms over her chest, widening her stance as she uttered the actress' name, almost begging him to argue with her.

"What? Are you serious?" The words spluttered

from his mouth in disbelief. Perhaps she had nothing to worry about after all. "I will not be touching *that* again, it was like shagging a Barbie doll, all plastic and fake." He visibly shuddered as his mind drifted over the thought of him and Stacey together. "She was a huge mistake from day one, although to be fair, I can't remember most of it. Spent most of those days off my fucking tits one way or another. I won't be revisiting that anytime soon." Jake moved in closer, decreasing the distance between him and Olivia. "You know that look is not a good one for you, Liv, baby." The corner of his mouth twitched up in a vague smirk as he tucked a strand of hair behind Olivia's ear. His fingers caressed her cheek.

"What look?" Olivia scowled, flicking at his hand, pushing him away. "The pissed off, humiliated one?"

"The green-eyed-monster-jealous look." Pulling her in tight to his chest as he chuckled, he planted a kiss on her forehead. "You know, Liv, you have nothing to worry about. I'd rather spend the rest of my days appreciating every inch of your sexy, very real body."

Olivia studied his face. Perhaps her life as she was coming to know it wasn't over yet just because Stacey Freeman showed up to the party. "If you say so." He wasn't completely off the hook. She'd seen the way he'd looked at her in the dining room. "Can we leave the bathroom now? It's kind of creeping me out that you're in the ladies'."

Taking hold of her hand, Jake led her from the public restroom and back to the table where Ben and Alex sat waiting. Olivia took in the sight of their joined hands as he guided her through the restaurant. For such a small gesture, handholding certainly went underrated. Sex was amazing - sex with Jake was even better - but handholding was a prelude to so much more. It led to kisses, caresses, and felt much more intimate than it actually was.

CHAPTER
Twenty-Four

The final night of the rescheduled tour had been a complete success. The guest appearances by Ben and Alex had been the highlight, sending the crowd into a frenzied mass. The thrill of seeing Jake on stage performing with two former members of Uni-Fi had blown everyone away. Jake felt on top of the world again, as though he was right back where he was always meant to be. It was as though his whole career, including the ups and downs, had been geared up to that final night. The extreme high he'd experienced beat any drug or alcohol-induced feelings of euphoria he'd had in the past. He'd left the arena that night feeling far more in control of his future than he had for a very long time. All he needed was for that to continue.

So why now they were home did he feel so useless? The wondering through the house aimlessly had begun less than twenty-four hours after they'd landed. The studio he was having built at the house was almost complete; the builders flitted around the property making their presence known to both Jake and Olivia. The intrusion was grating on him. His home didn't feel like his own. It should have been his haven, not some kind of free for all that it was at the minute.

"Liv!" Jake called down the hallway.

Olivia poked her head out from behind the laundry room door. "In here." She smiled at the sight of him walking barefoot down the corridor towards her. Her eyes drawn to his feet as he drew nearer. It should be illegal for feet to be considered sexy.

"What are you doing laundry for? I have someone to do that. That's not your job. We talked about this, babe." Wrapping his hand around the back of her head, he pulled her in quickly for a kiss, his tongue running along the seam of her lips until she opened for him. "Mmmm," he groaned as her tongue touched his.

"Sorry, mate. S'cuse us, just need to squeeze past you. Ta." One very large builder shimmied past Jake in the hallway, causing him to step closer into Olivia.

"That." Olivia pointed after the builder. "Is exactly why I'm in here. It's the only place I get any peace. They're either bugging me to sign off on some crap or all

I can hear is hammering and drilling. If I shut the door, I can just about concentrate on these emails." She waved a hand in the direction of the work surface where her tablet, phone, and paperwork were spread out.

Jake groaned. "They were supposed to be done before I got home. I can't stand all this going on while I'm here." He leaned in to kiss those delicious lips again. "You shouldn't have to hide in here, baby. Use the office upstairs." His mouth found that special place just below her ear. When he sucked lightly on the soft skin there, Olivia shuddered.

"Can't. They expect me to be in there and they'll find me. I'm hiding in here. Join me?" Grinning mischievously up at him, she gripped his T-shirt and yanked him forwards. Jake lost his footing and stumbled heavily into her, forcing her up against the washing machine behind her. "Close the door." Rising on her tiptoes, Olivia nipped at his bottom lip playfully as her fingers strained to find bare flesh beneath the fabric of his T-shirt.

Jake kicked out backwards, his foot connecting with the laundry room door to slam it shut behind him. "Impatient, are we?"

"You bet." Her arms snaked around his neck, pulling him in tighter to her body, her breasts pushing up against his chest, her hard nipples rubbing against him.

Lifting her up easily, Jake sat her on the edge of the worktop, forcing her legs to spread as he positioned himself in the space between her knees. "I like it when you wear a skirt. Gives me better access to you." With his hands firmly on her bottom, he pulled her swiftly forward, allowing her covered pussy to make contact with his groin. A low groan escaped Olivia's lips as Jake's hands roamed over the bare flesh of her thighs. Her hands gripped the hem of his shirt, pulling it up and off over his head, allowing her free access to his glorious bare chest. Jake let out a low hiss as she ran her fingers along the sensitive skin on his sides. Pushing up her top and pulling down the cups on her bra, Jake exposed her breasts. Lowering his mouth to one perfect rose-coloured nipple, his tongue darted out to lick the hard bud before sucking it into his mouth.

Olivia's hands became frenzied, fighting with the belt on his jeans and then the buttons. *Oh, thank the Lord for button fly jeans.* With one swift pull, they all popped open in unison. As she pushed the offending clothing down on his hips, Jake swept her thong aside before lining himself up with her pussy and driving home in one quick movement.

"Fuuuck." Olivia gasped as he pulled out to the

very tip and slammed back inside her again. With firm hands gripping her hips tightly, Jake carried on with a punishing, non-relenting rhythm.

"Baby, I'm close," Jake muttered, his eyes fixed on where their bodies were joined. Watching his cock slide in and out of her was the best view on earth.

"I need more." Lowering her hand, she began running circles around her clit as Jake fucked her. She felt the warm sensation begin to flood through her veins. Closing her eyes, she focused on reaching her goal when Jake unapologetically removed her hand.

"That's mine. I'll give you whatever you need, just come for me, baby." Jake's knuckle took over the job of circling her tight bundle of nerves, leaving Olivia to grip the worktop with both hands as her body soared. Jake rolled his hips, making sure he hit that special spot inside her, prolonging her pleasure as long as he could while he came long and hard inside her.

Slowing his movements, Jake waited until Olivia's breathing returned to near normal before he gently pulled out and tucked himself inside his clothing. Lifting his hands to hold her cheeks, his fingers slid into her hair, bringing her forward to kiss her lovingly. "How fast can you pack a bag?" He almost whispered against her lips.

"For what?"

"I need to get away from here while this is going on. Ben said we can use the beach house; they're not using it until after the baby arrives. He wants Iz near the hospital for D-Day." The last time he'd been at the house was for Ben and Izzie's surprise wedding. It was the most serene setting with hardly any neighbours, which certainly carried a huge amount of appeal. And more importantly, there was no building work going on. "These guys said they'll be here for about four more days, so I figured we could spend that time on the beach. I can work on some new material for the album while we're there. So, how fast can you pack a bag?"

Olivia smiled. "For me, five minutes. For you, it may take me a while. You're a little picky."

"Mine's packed and in the car. That's why I came to find you, but you trapped me in here and made me perform dirty sex acts on you." He pinched the tip of her nose gently as he teased her. Stepping backwards, he pulled open the laundry room door, indicating for her to exit first. "Go grab your things and I'll put this stuff in the car." Gathering up her paperwork, phone, and everything else he could see, he shuffled out behind her. "Go. The beach awaits."

CHAPTER
Twenty-Five

$\mathcal{N}$inety minutes later, Jake pulled the black Porsche Cayenne onto the drive of Ben and Izzie's beachfront property. As he turned off the engine, he turned to take in the sight of Olivia snoozing in the passenger seat beside him. She'd passed out around twenty minutes into the journey. Either he was boring company or she was worn out from the tour dates. Placing his large hand on her knee, he tenderly squeezed, trying to wake her gently. "Hey, sleepy head. We're here."

"Mmm..." Olivia's eyes blinked slowly open. "Sorry." Stretching out her arms, she looked around lazily at the view through the windscreen. The white-clad house sat to their right, leaving nothing but sand and ocean sprawling out before them. "Wow. That's one amazing view." Olivia let out a low whistle to further show her appreciation.

"It's pretty special, but just wait until you see inside the house. It's insane." Jake hopped out of the car, scooting around to open Olivia's door for her. Jake wasn't wrong; the house was beautiful inside and out. Each room had been newly decorated in a crisp fresh and light colour scheme. There were no trashy beach-themed rooms to be seen. Olivia wandered from room to room, leaving Jake to bring in their bags. The small covered balcony at the back of the house could quite possible be her new favourite place. The two Adirondack chairs sat side by side on the decking were positioned perfectly, overlooking the sea. That's where Jake found her sitting, lost in her own thoughts, oblivious to the fact that he'd even appeared beside her.

"You like?" he asked, smiling down at her as he handed her a hot coffee cup.

"Oh, I love. It's just perfect." Sipping on the almost molten liquid, her eyes never left the ocean. "I really love the sea. It's so tranquil, don't you think?"

"It's okay. I'm not the greatest swimmer so it kinda freaks me out a bit. Ben's a surfer, though, so he'd be on your level with the whole tranquil vibe." Jake settled into the chair beside her. Lifting his cup to his lips, he blew gently over the hot liquid. "He spent most of his summers here with his parents as a kid, I think. Pretty lucky childhood if you ask me, having this on your doorstep."

"Yeah, not your average childhood home, is it?" It was far removed from the home Olivia had grown up in. The suburban two up two down had been clean and comfortable but that was about the best thing she could say about her childhood home. "What was your house like? The one you grew up in, I mean."

"It was okay. Average at best. My parents worked hard to give us what we needed but we weren't rich or anything. My parents still live in the same house. They won't let me buy them anywhere nicer. I paid their mortgage off, though." He smiled at the memory. The look on his mum's face when he told her he'd cleared their debt had been priceless. It was his way of paying them back for everything they'd struggled through in order for him to succeed. It had been the best feeling ever when his dad had looked at him with nothing but pride in his eyes. Then the sadness hit, the shame that his father no longer looked at him with pride but instead shame or contempt.

"You don't talk about them much, your parents. In fact, that's the first time I've heard you mention them. I bet they're proud of you." Judging by the look on his face, that was completely the wrong thing to say.

"Proud? No, they're very much the opposite of

proud. At least, they were six months ago when they last spoke to me. They could be dead for all I know, although I'm sure someone would've let me know." His shoulders slumped forwards. The coffee cup cradled in his hands became his sole interest as he studied the liquid with intent. "They kinda disowned me." Olivia's sharp intake of breath startled him slightly. "Can't blame them, not really. I put them through hell when I was using. I was either wasted or shit-faced permanently." Jake risked a sideways look at his girlfriend, needing to judge how she was taking this news. He wasn't surprised she looked slightly appalled by his words. "I lied to them all the time. My dad knew long before my mum that I was an addict. He told me that if I couldn't stop then I wasn't welcome home anymore. They argued, mum cried, I punched my dad and broke his nose. It wasn't pretty. I was fucking wasted." Jake let his confession rest between them in the silence. Only the sound of the waves crashing against the shoreline interrupted them. "In my dad's words; I'm scum. They had to stand by and watch me come apart at the seams. It was probably the hardest thing they've ever had to do. I don't blame them. You shouldn't either."

"You are not scum, Jake Williams. You're not totally broken, just slightly bent out of shape, but nothing that cannot be fixed. Have you tried to contact them recently?" Olivia reached her hand out across the short distance, wrapping her fingers around his. She squeezed tightly, letting him know he wasn't alone anymore.

"Yeah, two weeks ago. I rang my mum but she sent it straight to voicemail. I left a message, told her I was clean and that I'd sent plane tickets for them to come see me in Germany at the last show. They didn't show up. I think that tells me all I need to know, don't you? I only ever wanted them to be proud of me but I fucked that up."

Olivia's heart ached for him. She knew right then that she was in love him. There was no denying it any longer. Despite every effort to protect her stupid heart, she'd gone and let him invade it wholly. She couldn't find the right words to answer him. Whatever she said, it wouldn't be the right thing. Not now, not ever. They were his parents and they'd abandoned him when he needed them most. She'd never make peace with that.

"Enough with this depressing shit." Standing, he pulled her to her feet. "If we walk along the shoreline there's a really great seafood restaurant. You hungry?" Right on cue, a loud rumble sounded from her stomach, causing them both to giggle. "I'll take that as a yes. Come on."

With their jeans rolled up to almost their knees, they walked barefoot along the water's edge, both of them clutching the other's hand tightly as they strolled towards the lights twinkling in the distance. The smell of food had begun to waft over the bay towards them, increasing their hunger.

As they reached the hidden bay, Maxwell's restaurant illuminated the cove with its softly glowing, candle lit tables outside underneath the awning.

Jake handed over a menu. "The tails are amazing, but pick whatever." Olivia's eyes perused the food as the waitress carried it out to waiting patrons. She didn't need a menu as the plates that kept passing her looked mouth-watering. It was a much better indication of what was on offer than peering at a list in a folder, she always found.

"What can I get you guys, tonight? We have tuna on special, or the clam chowder is always popular." The sunny-looking waiter smiled down with his pen poised to take their order. "What's in those big silver buckets?" Olivia pointed to the table next door.

"That's our surfer's special. You get the tails, tempura prawns, squid and crab claws."

"I'll have that, please, and a water. Thanks." She smiled. Jake ordered the lobster tails and a beer before handing back his own menu. He could feel Olivia bristling from across the table but she had the sense to keep quiet until the waiter had left the table. "Jake."

"The beer is for you, not me. Liv, you don't have to spend the rest of your life with me avoiding alcohol. I can sit here and be fine while you have a beer. It's not a big deal, baby." Reaching across the table, he took her hand in his, caressing her palm with his fingertips. "When he brings your water, we'll just switch."

Olivia tried to protest but he put a stop to it instantly. "Please. I don't like it when you try to protect me from it. You couldn't stop me if I wanted to drink, so please, just let me do this my way, okay?"

"Okay." It didn't mean she had to feel comfortable with it, though. When the waiter placed the bottle before Jake, she saw the look in his eyes. She knew how hard it was for him, so without a word, she picked up their drinks and simply swapped them around. "Change of plan." She smiled up at the waiter. "My date is driving now instead of me."

As the tension eased from the situation, Jake began to relax again. "So, tell me more about Liv the teenager."

"Nothing much to tell you that I haven't already spilled. You know all about my dad-"

"No, not him. I want to hear about you. You don't talk about any friends or family, any ties back home, or even where home really is. So, tell me, who is Olivia Holmes?"

"Again, not much to tell you. I was a loner, preferred to hide in my room with a book more than anything else. I didn't do the whole party thing, or the teenage angst bit either. I kept my head down and kept out of the way." Olivia picked at the crab claws with a long fork type thing, pulling out the flesh from inside as she spoke. "As for friends, I didn't really have any."

"You must have had friends!" Jake snorted. "Everybody has friends growing up."

"Not when your father is an alcoholic who spends his days passed out in his underwear on the sofa at home, you don't. I learnt from an early age that nobody else's dad drank whiskey with their cereal in the morning. It's not the kinda thing you want the girls in your class to see, is it?" Olivia continued to tuck into her bucket of seafood, not realising for a minute or two that Jake had stopped eating. He sat opposite her, watching her hands pick over the shells and flesh, deciding which to tuck into next. When the silence hit her, she looked up to see him staring at her.

"What did I do?" Olivia spoke around a mouthful of lobster tail.

"Nothing." He beamed as he watched her chew. "I love that you just spoke about your dad's addiction in front of me, without trying to flower it up or make it sound anything other than it was. I also love that you're still sitting here with me, even though I'm an addict. You're not letting your past affect us. I love that, that's all I was thinking."

"Ex-addict. You keep forgetting that bit. You're no longer an addict. That's why I'm here."

"I love you." Jake spoke clearly, never had he been surer of anything. "I'm in love with you. Don't freak out. You don't have to say it back, I didn't say it just so you'd say it back to me." Jake watched the fear hit Olivia's eyes. Lifting the beer to her lips, she tipped it backwards and chugged down almost all of the remaining liquid as she tried to give herself a minute of composure. "Liv, it's fine, baby. Calm down. I only said I love you, I didn't ask you to marry me. Breathe."

"Will you stop saying that? You don't know me. You can't love me."

"Who says I can't? I'm not under the influence of any substance, I'm sober, so yeah, I know how I feel about you." Olivia stared open-mouthed at him, she could see his mouth moving so knew there must be words coming out, what those words were; she had no idea. "I also know you love me back, but I think that's taking things a little far for tonight's chat." Jake smirked as Olivia spluttered and coughed around her food. "Shall I just pay the bill? You wanna go back?" He could barely contain his laughter at the dismayed look on her face.

Olivia only nodded before forcing down the remainder of her beer.

CHAPTER Twenty-Six

atching Jake work peacefully from the deck, Olivia pondered over the last night's revelations. It had taken a fair few hours and more gentle words of encouragement from Jake for her to finally calm down about his declarations of love. No, she hadn't said the words back to him but that wasn't because she didn't feel them. More that she needed to make peace with them first. She did love him, she was almost sure of that. But just then she had a job to do; that had to come first.

Opening up her emails, she scrolled through her emergency contacts list for Jake. What she was about to do could cost her dearly but she knew she couldn't let it rest. Not without at least giving it a shot. Maybe, just maybe, she could help to fix him. With one final check over the top of her laptop to make certain he was still busy with his guitar, Olivia brought up the contact details of one Mrs Helen Williams – Jake's mother. Olivia saw no point in going to his father; she figured that wouldn't be her wisest move, but there was a bond between mothers and sons that surely could still be repaired with a gentle nudge in the right direction. She'd risk going all the way to hell and back for this if it meant he gained some peace.

"What're you doing?" Jake peered over the top of her laptop, trying to catch a glimpse of what she was typing.

Snapping the lid shut as she jumped, Liv looked sheepishly at him. "Nothing. Just sending Izzie some work stuff. How's the new material going?" She knew that was a sure fire way to distract him. Whenever he got started with the guitar, it was hard to drag him away again.

"Great. Do you wanna hear some?" He sat next to her and begun strumming out a tune before she could answer. With his eyes focused on the strings, he played the opening chords of a new track before starting to sing a few lines of lyrics he'd written that afternoon. "That's all I've got at the minute, needs a bit of polishing in the studio, but Dave will work his magic on it. What do you think?" With excited eyes, he waited for her response.

"I love it. It's old-school-Jake. Sounds great."

Olivia's email pinged, alerting her to a new message. She hesitated opening it in case it was his mother rejecting him again. But no, it was only Izzie informing her the builders would be around for another few days. "They've hit a cable, apparently. Izzie says to stay holed up here for a few more days." Lifting her gaze to the view she added, "Although I'm not about to complain if I get to carry on looking at that for a while longer."

They spent the rest of the hazy afternoon out on the deck, with Jake picking out tunes on his guitar then scribbling notes in a book while Olivia dangled her feet over the edge of the deck, drawing loose circles in the sand below. As the sun set, everything around them became tinged with a warm purple haze. A light breeze blew in from across the ocean, ruffling Olivia's long hair as it nestled around her shoulders. Jake dropped a warm throw cover over her shoulders as he lowered himself onto the deck beside her. "I'm gonna drive over to Maxwell's and pick up some food. Any requests, or should I just grab a bit of everything?"

Making to stand up, Olivia offered to go with him. "Just give me two minutes."

"Nah, stay here and watch the sunset. I'll be thirty minutes, tops." He kissed the top of her head before he climbed into the car and revved the engine then pulled away into the road. Snuggling further inside the cosy throw cover, Oliva wrapped it tightly around her shoulders and settled back to watch as the sun disappeared below the ocean. It wasn't until it completely disappeared and the chill really set in that she realised how long she'd been sitting there. Glancing at her watch, she realised it had been almost two hours since Jake had left to pick up food. An all too familiar feeling swam around her stomach as she scrambled to her feet. Retrieving her phone from the small outdoor table, she hit Jake's number. Listening to it ring out against her ear did nothing to calm her nerves. When it went to voicemail, she hung up and hit redial. Still no answer.

"Shit. Shit. Shit. Fucking shit. Where the hell are you?" she muttered to herself as she paced up and down the deck. Googling the number for Maxwell's, she decided they were her next point of call. After she described Jake's appearance to them, they assured her he hadn't been in all night. Cutting the call off, Olivia stared at the screen, and the picture of her and Jake together stared back at her. It had been taken when they were in Germany on the morning they spent shopping at the plaza before he'd found out Graham had tried to sabotage him. They both looked happy. Jake's smile was the most natural she'd ever seen it in that picture and now she had no idea where he was or if he was safe. Why the hell had she let him go alone? Her only job was to keep him safe and away from temptation and now she'd allowed him be exposed to his demons. She'd let him down.

Hitting the screen again, she dialled his number and waited, but again there was no answer, it just went straight to voicemail. "Jake, where are you? Call me back please, just let me know you're okay." Hanging up again, she began to rationalise with herself. If he wasn't back in thirty minutes, she'd ring Izzie and casually ask if she'd spoken to Jake. No need to panic her, but at least then she'd know if he'd been in contact with Izzie. Yes, that's what she'd do. Who the hell was she trying to convince? She couldn't ring Izzie. What the hell was she supposed to say? *'Hey, has Jake rung you because I appear to have lost him.'* Yeah, that'd go down really well. Pacing up and down the deck again, she peered out into the dark sky, trying to come up with a plan of action. The police. She'd ring them if he wasn't back in the next few minutes. They'd at least know if there'd been any accidents or if he was lying in a ditch somewhere. So help him if he wasn't, she'd sure as hell put him there if he waltzed through that door in the next few minutes, large as life with some crappy excuse. No, she wouldn't. She'd run into his arms and tell him she loved him, just like she should have done already. "Come on, Jake. Where are you?"

The fear in her stomach rolled and pitched like a bitch. Heading inside the house, she wrapped the throw tighter around her shoulders, the uncertainty making her shiver even more. Perched on the edge of the kitchen barstool, Olivia clutched a glass of water between her hands as she watched the clock tick from one minute to the next. He'd been gone for a couple of hours. A lot can happen in that time. Why was she waiting any longer? He was missing and she needed to find him. Picking up the phone again, she dialled the emergency service number and waited for an answer. When the operator asked her which service she required, Olivia managed to hold it together and explain the situation. The police officer she eventually got to speak to didn't seem that concerned that a grown man had been MIA for four hours, especially when she explained exactly who Jake was. "I understand, Ms Holmes, but to be honest, until he's been gone for twenty-four hours, there's not much we can do. I'll give you my number. If he shows up before then just give me a call. He's probably lost track of time in some bar somewhere. He'll be home before you know it."

Wasn't that the problem? Jake in a bar was not a great idea. She only had one option left. She had to phone Izzie. Checking the time, she knew Izzie would know instantly that something was wrong if she rang at this time of night, but what other choice did she have? None. Nada. She'd drawn a blank and Jake still wasn't home. He could be anywhere, but Olivia was more worried he was drunk and it was all her fault.

Izzie answered on the third ring. "What's happened?" Her voice sounded tight, the concern simmering just beneath the surface.

"I've lost him." Izzie choked out the words around a sob. "I don't know where he is, he's been gone hours. I'm sorry."

"Shit! What the fuck did you do?" Izzie almost growled down the phone.

"I... nothing. He went out for food. He never came back."

"I'm getting in the car. Stay there, he may turn up. How long's he been gone?"

"Two hours."

"Fucking hell, Olivia." The line went dead, leaving Olivia to sob alone.

CHAPTER
Twenty-Seven

The front door swung open, banging against the hallway wall, causing the small console table to vibrate somewhat. Jake fell through the doorway, tripping over the small step that led into the entrance. "Yeah, thanks, mate." Jake turned to call over his shoulder, his right arm raised to someone outside, his left hand grasping the doorframe tightly as he wobbled slightly.

Liv shot out of the kitchen, wiping her damp cheeks on the cuffs of her sleeves. "Jake? Oh, thank Christ." She covered the short distance down the hallway in seconds, her hands reaching out to check he was actually standing there. "Where the hell have you been? You've been gone hours."

"Don't." Jake shrugged his arms out of her grasp. "Fuckin' touch." His words slurred slightly, his speech slow and steady to match his pace as he bravely let go of the doorframe to push past her towards the kitchen. She could see he was drunk but plainly trying to appear as though he wasn't.

Liv looked outside through the front door before closing it quietly. His car wasn't there. She didn't know whether to be relieved he hadn't driven, or worried as to what he'd done with the Porsche. She followed him into the kitchen and watched as he searched through cabinets, looking for something. "Where's the car?"

"Eh?" The rummaging continued. "Oh, car. Yeah. Dunno."

"You don't know where you left the car?" The skin on Liv's arms began to prickle through apprehension. "Is it at Maxwell's?"

"Why you so fuckin' interested all of a sudden?" Doors continued to slam as he carried on searching for what Liv presumed was alcohol.

"Because it's your car. You can't just lose your car, Jake!" She tried desperately to keep her voice calm but it was starting to betray her. Moving closer to him, she placed her hand on top of his to stop him from decimating the kitchen cabinets. Jake froze, his eyes fixed on the hand that rested on top of his as though it was burning right through him. "Look, we can find the car tomorrow. Why don't I make you some coffee then I'll phone Izzie and let her know you're home safe-"

Jake whipped his hand out from beneath hers, causing her to stumble slightly at the rage she felt between them. "You fuckin' rang her too? You fuckin' stupid bitch. Is she on her way here? That's all I fuckin' need."

"I didn't know where you were! I was worried and you didn't answer your phone!" The words came out rushed and panicked. Jake's eyes had glassed over, becoming cold and even angrier than they already were. "I'll phone her, tell her you're fine. Don't worry, I'll sort it out." Liv reached for her phone on the countertop but Jake got there first. Sweeping it away from her reach, he picked it up and tried to unlock the screen.

"I wonder who else you rang today. Shall we check?" He swayed slightly on the spot as he tried to concentrate on unlocking the phone. "Piece shit, fuckin' thing not opening." Waving it in front of her, he continued to taunt her. "Don't matter, we both know what ya did." His speech was becoming more slow and purposeful as he tried not to slur his words.

"Wha- I didn't do anything. Jake, you're not making sense. Why don't you go up to bed and I'll clean up down here and be up in a minute, yes?" Liv snatched her phone from his barely clenched fist.

"With you? Not a fucking chance." He turned his

back on her. Leaving the kitchen, he made his way towards the stairway.

"I spoke to my dad tonight. He rang just as I got to the restaurant. Funny that, donchya think?" Jake paused at the bottom of the stairs "That he'd just call, outta nowhere." He turned slightly to face Liv again. A small amount of spit ran out of the corner of his mouth as he struggled to form his lips around the words. "Oops, it wasn't outta nowhere. I forgot, you emailed them, didn't ya?" Fixing Liv with a stare, he crossed his arms over his chest. As he tried to widen his stance on the step, his foot missed, causing him to slip and lose his balance, ending up on his arse at the bottom of the staircase. "Fuckin'. Hell!" He slammed his fists hard into the floor beside him.

Liv rushed over to his side, crouching beside him to help gather him up. "Get the fuck way. Done enough damage." He waved his arms around in big sweeping movements. Liv had no choice but to get out of his way, he'd have knocked her over otherwise. If she could only get him upright and up the stairs to bed before Izzie arrived, maybe then this wouldn't be such a disaster. He struggled to his feet, hanging onto the stair rail with a death like grip to enable him to remain upright. "They hate me. My parents fuckin' hate me. You had to dig that up again." Jake staggered closer to

Liv. His warm, beer-soaked breath assaulted her senses, forcing her to turn her head away before she gagged at the stench. One finger poked at her chest repeatedly, punctuating his words as he continued his onslaught. "Couldn't leave it, couldya? Fucking. Stupid. Bitch."

"Jake..."

"Shutthefuckup!" His words scrambled as his hands came to rest on her shoulders, gripping tightly. Liv didn't know if he was trying to scare her or just steady himself against her. She was hoping it was the latter but the knot in her stomach was trying to tell her differently.

"I'm dead, that's what he said. Dead. They don't have a son no more. Ya think I really need to hear that again? Nope. I was happy kinda not hearin' it again."

"You're hurting me, Jake." Olivia tried to free his hands from her shoulders but he wouldn't let go. "Jake, let go, please." Her small fingers tried to wriggle underneath his to loosen his grip.

"I'm hurtin' you?" He snorted, spraying her face with spit. "You fuckin' destroyed me tonight. Oh, and I had a little drink too." Releasing one shoulder, he held up his hand in front of her face, his forefinger and thumb showing a small gap between them. "Jus' the one." His mouth curled up at the corner as he tried not to laugh.

"I think you had more than one. Did you take anything?" She really didn't want to hear the answer but knew she needed to know what she was dealing with.

Jake's eyes glassed over again, shutting her out. "Is that what's important here, if I scored or not?" His icy words cut through her. He let go of her other shoulder, turning to leave, but on a whim swung around, flailing his arms around as he turned. The back of one of his hands collided with Olivia's cheek. The slapping sound rang out in the silence between them.

Olivia's hand instinctively rose to her face, her palm cupping her cheek as the sting of both humiliation and pain rang through her. "You hit me. You fucking hit me," she whispered.

"Shit. Not on purpose, don't be a fucking drama queen. Let me see." Jake steadied himself on his feet. Leaning forward, he tried to pry her hand away from her face so he could assess the damage.

With all the force she could muster, Olivia pushed hard on Jake's chest, sending him backwards towards the staircase again. "Do. Not. Touch. Me. Again." He stumbled and landed in a jumble on the bottom step. "Too far, Jake. Too far." Picking up her coat from the end of the bannister, she walked towards the front door.

Taking a second to pause, she glanced back over her shoulder at the mess that was now Jake Williams, crumpled and broken at the bottom of the staircase. Email or no email, booze or no booze, there was no way she was sticking around to be anyone's punch bag.

"Liv," Jake called out solemnly down the hallway.

"No. You're an adult. You're capable of making good choices in life. I think you need to start doing that now. I'm done, I told you I'd only stay while you were sober."

CHAPTER
Twenty-Eight

hen Olivia left the beach house, she had no idea where she was heading, she just knew she wouldn't, *couldn't* go back inside. There was nothing left in there for her now. She couldn't be around another drunk, stepping on eggshells and not knowing what the next day would bring. She also had no clue how long Jake had been left on his own or if he'd passed out in his own vomit.

But that had been three days ago. Those three days had been difficult. After leaving the beach house, Olivia had called a taxi from the end of the street and asked to go to the station where she'd bought a ticket to the seaside town of Crosston. It was the next train to leave; she'd figured it was a big enough town to get lost in. And she'd probably be able to find a job there too, seeing as she'd just fucked hers up. The bed and break-fast she'd found a room in was clean, tidy, and seemed fairly reputable. At least they didn't seem to rent rooms out by the hour. Well, not that she'd noticed yet, anyway.

As she sat on the bed in the small single room, the screen on her phone lit up with yet another text message. Sighing deeply, she tapped on the icon to read it.

"Hey, how are you doing? Please call me. I'm sorry and I miss you. X"

It was the latest in a long line of messages from Jake. They'd started twelve hours after she'd walked out on him. Izzie had rung first, which Liv hadn't answered either, but she'd at least told her that Jake was okay, he was hooked up with his counsellor again, and she also said she didn't blame Liv, that her job was still open if she still wanted it. The only explanation was that Jake was, in fact, sober and had managed to calm her down. God only knows he had her wrapped around his finger at the best of times. Izzie had every right to blame her for Jake's lapse, she'd been the one who'd lost track of time, she'd let him go out alone to a place she knew sold alcohol. If only she could turn back the clock, she'd replay that night so differently.

She'd never have sent the email in the first place. Izzie might say she didn't blame her but Olivia certainly blamed herself. She couldn't see how she could go back. Nor did she want to. Her days of living with an alcoholic were over, they ended when her father died. Jake had said it himself; he'd always be an addict. Now she knew she wasn't the one to fix him. Only he could do that for himself but he needed to want to get better first.

Olivia read over the message one more time before deleting it. Just as she had the hundred other messages. She wasn't into self-torture, and re-reading them would be exactly that. From now on it was onwards and upwards, no going back. Pushing the phone inside her bag, Olivia slipped her coat on and set out on her daily job hunt. There was a bar in town that had been advertising for staff; there was no harm in trying.

"Where the fuck is she?" Jake pounded his fists on Izzie's desk. "She's been gone three days. Three fucking days. She could be on the other side of the world by now." He paced up and down the hard wooden floor of his manager's office, his hands gripping his hips as he went. "Why won't she at least let one of us know she's safe? She doesn't have to come back to me, I just need to know she's safe, Iz."

Izzie ran her thumb and forefinger over the bridge of her nose. "You hurt her. She saw you at your worse. She's protecting herself, that's all. You're just going to have to give her some time to calm down." Pushing back in her chair, Izzie studied the young man who she'd known for years, watched him grow up in the business, and watched this business try to destroy him. He was like a younger brother to her. She would do anything to make sure he made it back again this time. "You know, this is why we have a 'no fraternisation' clause built into the employment contract. It's for your own good. It was meant to protect you from all this... shit."

"Liv is not the shit I need protecting from. I'm the only thing I need protecting from. Just me." He slumped down in the chair opposite Izzie. "I'm going to try calling her again."

"No, just leave her alone for a bit. Give her some space. Maybe she'll contact one of us then."

"I can't fucking leave it! I said some pretty shitty things to her and I hit her. I need to make that right. She needs to listen to me so I can make it right." Getting up from the chair, Jake made his way to the large floor to ceiling window that overlooked the city he'd come to call home. "I'm going to drive back up to the beach house, have a drive around there again. Maybe she stayed local…"

"Jake, she's more likely to have gone home, back to her family, friends. That'd make more sense but we drove around there and no luck, so…"

"That's the last place she'd go. She doesn't go back, only forwards." He left out the part about her dad; that wasn't his story to tell. If Olivia wanted anyone to know about her father she had to be the one to tell them.

"Jake, you can't just go driving around the coast-line for hours on end, hoping you might bump into her like star-crossed lovers from some crappy romance movie! It's a really stupid idea."

"Fucking watch me." Flinging the door open, Jake headed out of the office towards the main entrance. Izzie had located his car outside a bar half a mile away from the beach house. Ben had driven up and down the streets for an hour looking for it. Thankfully it was only a small village without very many streets to trawl along. It didn't hurt that the Porsche stuck out like a sore thumb either. Once Jake had sobered up, Ben had taken him to collect it, and they'd all driven back the next day.

As he started the engine up, his phone alerted him to an incoming text. He prayed to anyone that would listen it was from Olivia, but no, it was Izzie asking him to keep her up to date. He fired off a reply before he pulled the car out onto the main road and flicked the radio on. Imagine Dragons' *Not Today* echoed from the speakers as he pushed his foot down harder on the gas pedal.

He'd exhausted every inch within a five mile radius of the beach house, he'd searched every guest house and café he could find, left no corner of beach unsearched, but still she didn't want to be found. Sitting on the pebbled beach, Jake watched as the tide began to turn, creeping further up the shoreline towards him. It wouldn't be long before it was lapping at his feet. He'd lost track of time sitting there, but he somehow felt closer to her while sitting on the beach. It was as though it had become their place, even though they'd only spent a short time there together, and it was where he'd broken her heart. It had to get easier somehow.

If she was out there, he was going to find her, and when he did, he'd make a memory out of all of this heartache.

CHAPTER
Twenty-Nine

s each day passed, it became easier to move on. Keeping her mind occupied and off a certain rock star had become her priority. Keeping busy was the best medicine, but without a job, that was difficult. Almost three weeks had gone by since walking out on Jake. Most of those days had been spent walking along the beach or through the village. They normally ended in spending a few hours holed up in a coffee shop before making her way back to the guest house for the night. Olivia knew that the time to make a decision about her future was drawing nearer; avoiding it for too much longer really wasn't an option. The money she'd saved from working for Jake wouldn't last forever. She'd need somewhere to live, then a new job.

Sitting in The Fat Angel, sipping on a bottle of beer, was not going to solve any of her problems, this she knew, but it sure beat the hell out of sitting alone in that tiny guest house bedroom. She'd perfected the art of making a couple of bottles last late into the evening. The bustle of the bar kept her mind occupied, but she couldn't help wondering how Jake was doing. She prayed he was still on plan, sticking with the counselling and getting stronger. Although, Olivia knew it was a day-by-day fight. Hell, most days it was hour by hour. The ache in her chest still served as a reminder of what she'd left behind, the possibilities of what they could've been together. But all that was gone. She'd face the uncertain future alone if she had to. She wasn't afraid to move on with her life if that's what was needed.

Olivia turned her attention back towards the window, watching as people scurried past, carrying out their everyday tasks. The bar was getting busier as the night drew in. The clientele changed slowly from the casually dressed afternoon drop-ins, to the smartly dressed office dwellers starting their weekends off with a swift drink on their way home from work.

Dropping a bottle of beer in front of her, the bartender smiled. "Compliments of the guy at the end of the bar." Leaning in a little, he lowered his voice. "I opened it. It's not spiked so you're safe, although the guy who bought it is old enough to be your dad, just so you know."

Olivia rolled her eyes at the barman. "Send it back. Tell him thanks, but no thanks." Pushing the bottle of beer back towards the bemused server, Olivia grabbed her bag and threw it over her shoulder before turning to leave the comfort of the bar.

"Liv." One strong hand grabbed her forearm, stopping her in her tracks. "Don't rush off. Here, sit with me and at least drink the beer I bought you." Olivia turned to see Andy standing next to her, his hand still on her arm. When her eyes rested on his fingers in irritation, he released her immediately. "Please. It's just a beer."

"Is he here with you? Jake, I mean." Olivia's eyes darted around the now overcrowded bar, panic rising in her chest. If she saw him there was a chance her resolve would break. She couldn't see him but that didn't mean he wasn't hiding out somewhere, having sent Andy in to do his dirty work.

"No, he isn't here. It's just me. I promise." Andy pulled up a second bar stool and sat down, hoping Olivia would do the same.

With one final glance around the bar to satisfy herself that he was, in fact, alone, Olivia sat back down. Lifting the bottle to her lips, she took a tentative sip, all the time peering over the bottle at Andy. Jake's head of security wasn't there by accident. She wasn't that stupid. "Did he send you to find me?" For the most part, she wanted him to say yes, but realistically, she knew that wasn't a good thing either. If Jake really wanted her, he'd have come to find her himself.

"Not in so many words, no."

"What the hell does that mean? He either did or he didn't." Olivia turned to face Andy squarely. Her cover had been blown. There was no point in playing the wallflower anymore. "How is he?" It almost felt like an afterthought but she knew it wasn't. It was the only thing she wanted to know from the second she'd set eyes on Andy.

"Truthfully?" Andy searched her face for some kind of glimmer of hope. "He's sober. And clean."

"That's good. Really good then." Olivia smiled with relief.

"He may be sober but he's not in a good place. He is in hell on earth at the minute."

"It's early days. He'll settle down once the cravings settle again. That's all it is."

"No, it's you." Andy waited for her response, but when none came, he continued. "He's spent every day since you walked out looking for you. He's either on the phone texting or trying to call you, or he's driving around random towns and streets hoping to spot you." Taking a glug of his beer to quench his dry mouth, Andy let his words settle. "He rang every emergency department in a fifty mile radius that first few days. Not Izzie or some other minion in the office. Jake rang every damned one himself. Do you still have your work phone?"

Digging in her pocket, Olivia pulled out the phone Izzie had given her, holding it up to prove she'd still got it. "I read the first couple of texts and one from Izzie letting me know he was okay."

"He's not okay. That's not a word I'd use to describe his current state. Stressed, worried, angry even, are all better words." Olivia's features almost crumpled before him. "Look, I'm not saying you didn't do the right thing by walking out. You did. He needed to know you won't put up with his crap but, honestly, he deserves to know that you're still alive, at least."

"You can tell him." Sipping down more of the beer, Olivia avoided Andy's disapproving stare.

"Don't you think you owe him that much?"

"He hit me! I owe him nothing. He got drunk and hit me, Andy. What would you have done?"

"You know he wouldn't hurt you. It was an accident. He said it was an accident. Hey, I don't agree with men who hit women, all I'm saying is that wasn't

Jake. Not that night. You know that, and so do I. He's beating himself up over every last detail of that night. We've all lived through it time and time again with him. But you're not entirely innocent in all this either, are you? You contacted his mum, for crying out loud. That guy is one piece of shit excuse for a father. If you ask me, Jake's better off without him. You should've left that well alone. Maybe then we wouldn't all be in this mess." Olivia couldn't argue with that; she had been the one to try contacting his family, but she'd done it with the best intentions. Jake deserved to have his family in his life. He had been making good progress with his rehabilitation; they deserved to know that.

"Do you love him?" Andy questioned her. Throwing it out there into the open was the only way he could see to make her understand the enormity of the situation. "Because if you feel anything at all for him, then you should call him at least."

"And what if I don't love him? What then?"

"Then call him and tell him that. At least he'll know you're alive. He'll also know that it's time to move on. Get his mind back on his career, move forward. I dunno. But he deserves better than being left in limbo." Lifting his hand, Andy signalled the bartender to bring two more bottles of beer over. He wasn't about to give up yet. "Just needs a couple of words, Liv. If I go back and tell him I've seen you, he'll just come looking for you. If you don't want to be with him, that's up to you, but you need to tell him so he can start to heal. How do you feel about him?"

Tipping the bottle up, Olivia allowed the amber liquid to wash into her mouth as she glugged it down almost too quickly. "How did you find me?"

"By accident. My mother lives about three streets away from here. I came in for a drink before heading home for the weekend. I wasn't even sure it was you at first." Andy gave her the first genuine smile she'd seen in days. "You haven't answered my question. How do you feel about Jake?"

"It's got nothing to do with how I feel about him." Olivia blew out a long breath, as she signalled for another drink. "And more to do with not feeling those things for anybody else. What the fuck am I supposed to do? If I go back, what has he learnt? If I stay away, I'm hurting both of us. Right now, I don't want to be an adult, I want to be small again and have someone tell me what to do." She laughed at the thought.

"I can't tell you what to do, nobody can, but what I will say is this. He's in love with you, so you need to decide what you want. It's not fair to leave him hanging." Draining the rest of his beer from the bottle,

Andy stood up from his stool. "I should get going. Call me if you need anything. Jake doesn't need to know we talked."

Olivia tipped her chin in acknowledgement. She didn't have the words to speak. She barely managed to hold it together while Andy left the bar. The urge to run after him, begging him to take her to Jake was strong, but she needed to sort her feelings out first. Andy was right in that respect; she at least owed him that much. If she wasn't sure what she wanted or needed from him, how the hell was he supposed to know?

CHAPTER
Thirty

For the last three days, Olivia had picked up the phone to call Jake no less than a hundred times, but not once had she managed to go through with the actual call. Andy had really gotten under her skin. The sane, rational, sensible side of her told her she'd done exactly the right thing to cut all ties and walk away. The problem was, she'd never been the sort of person to do the right thing. Only right then, she couldn't decide what the right thing was. Her feelings for him hadn't altered - she was in love with him - but she wouldn't stick around and watch him destroy his life through any kind of abuse. She also wouldn't be his punch bag. One slap had been one too many. Hell, she was the girl who watched all the trashy daytime shows while shouting at the women to leave their partners. But she knew Jake wouldn't hurt her, he wasn't like that. If she was being totally honest with herself, she knew the slap had been purely accidental. She had been caught in the backlash as he swung around, nothing more. He hadn't purposely hit her.

She had a lot to think about, but she knew for sure that she was still in love with him, and if she could gain a fraction of the love back from him, then maybe it was worth risking it all.

Sliding her feet into her Converse, Olivia grabbed her coat and bag from the back of the bedroom door. If she was doing this, she was doing it now. No leaving time to talk herself out of it yet again. As she closed the front door to the guest house, she felt a sudden pang of nerves settle deep in her stomach. What if he didn't want to see her? What if he wasn't even there?

"Stop it!" she told herself as she began the brisk walk to the train station. She'd spent three days checking out the train timetables. If her memory served her correctly, she'd only have to wait a short time until she could board.

She'd made the train with thirty minutes to spare, bagging one of the few remaining seats. Settling into the window seat, she plugged in her earphones, allowing the music to drift through her, calming her as the motion of the train pacified the butterflies that were currently trying to break out of her stomach.

The butterflies had only just settled into some sort of gentle formation when the train drew to a standstill in London. Her stop. It was now or never. Gathering her thoughts Olivia stood to exit the train. When her feet hit the platform, the doubts ran amok through her brain. Mustering up all her stamina, she forced the niggles back down, pushing them aside as she forced her feet to propel her through the station towards the exit. Climbing in the rear of the first cab, Olivia reeled off Jake's address before sitting back to watch the bustling city pass by the window as they headed out towards the leafier parts of suburbia.

When the cab stopped outside the house, Olivia's stomach picked that moment to rise up her body as it tried to make its own escape. Swallowing hard, Olivia paid the fare before exiting the car. She stood stock still before the large gated property. With a deep breath, she crossed the road, making her way up towards the front door. Jake's car wasn't in the driveway, but her battered old heap still stood there. Fumbling for her keys, she wasn't sure if she should let herself in or knock and wait. She opted for the latter. It seemed only fair that she didn't take him by surprise. When the door swung open, she was greeted by the cleaner. Relief washed through her.

"Olivia! Oh, come in, come in. Jake isn't here but

you can wait." The door swung wide open as Maggie stood aside, beckoning her through.

"Thanks, but if he isn't here, I won't come in. I... maybe I'll come back later, okay?" Olivia smiled meekly at the poor confused woman.

"He's only at Izzie's. I can call him to come home. Really, come in."

"No, no. I'll come back later. Don't call him, it's fine, seriously." Turning, Olivia fished around in her bag again, this time pulling out the keys to her trusty old car. "I only came to collect my car anyway." She waved the keys aloft as if to prove her point.

As Maggie opened her mouth to speak again, Olivia dived inside her now unlocked car and prayed to anyone who would listen that it would start first time. "Come on, you heap of shit! Don't do this to me." As if sensing her need, the car fired first time, albeit with a cough of smoke. Ramming it into reverse, she lifted her hand in a wave goodbye as she backed down the driveway and out onto the road. Would she come back later? Well, that was anybody's guess.

Heading into the kitchen, Jake slung his keys on the countertop before switching on the coffee machine. His afternoon at Izzie's had been spent working out some new material with Ben, and his head was swimming with new lyrics. He'd not been able to focus much since Olivia had left, but today had been a good day. Finally he felt as though he could put something good together, something worth working on. All the angst he'd felt for the last month finally seemed to be pouring itself into his music.

"Hey, Maggie. I thought you'd be done by now. Did I leave the house that messy?" Jake smiled as his cleaner walked through from the laundry room.

"No more than usual, Jake, but I hung around until you got back." Placing the folded laundry on the counter, Maggie avoided his stare. He could see she had something to say but didn't know where to start.

"Look, if you broke something it's really not a problem. We've been over-"

"Olivia was here." Maggie blurted out the words quickly, still not daring to look at him.

"What?"

"She was here, not that long ago actually. She wouldn't come in or let me call you. Said she'd only come for her car..." The realisation that he hadn't noticed Olivia's car missing from the driveway hit him hard, forcing the air from his lungs.

"Why didn't you ring me? I was five minutes away, for fuck's sake! Maggie, I could've talked to her, begged her to listen to me, anything." His hands flew into his hair, tugging at the sides as he paced back and forth.

"I told you, she asked me not to. She was here and then she was gone. I didn't have time to call you."

"You didn't have time? You couldn't call me when she was here but you waited how long until I got home to tell me! You should've rung me the second she left. You said it wasn't that long ago. How long exactly?"

"Ten minutes, maybe slightly more. Really, not that long."

"Long enough. She took her car. She could be fucking miles away again. Thanks." Jake stormed from the kitchen, slamming the door behind him. Dragging his phone from his pocket, he dialled Olivia's number, praying she'd answer this time. When it went straight to voicemail he almost threw his phone against the wall.

CHAPTER Thirty-One

*P*eering out of the window, Jake could see her sitting there in her car. She hadn't moved for at least five minutes. He couldn't work out if that was a good thing or not, but at least she hadn't driven away again. He watched, mesmerised by her as she worried away at her hands. She was obviously contemplating her next move. Would she come into the house or would she start the car and leave again? He didn't want to call it either way. He'd stopped himself from running straight out there the minute he saw her pull up because he knew it had to be her choice. Just where he'd found that strength from was anyone's guess.

Olivia lifted her head and gazed up at the house. Jake's house. He probably wasn't even in; he was probably still out at Izzie's or in some bar getting wasted. She still wasn't convinced he was sober, despite Andy insisting he was; he was the hired help, after all. Letting out a long slow breath, Olivia lowered her head, resting it on the steering wheel as she considered her options. Options; like she really had any at all. There was nothing left at home for her now; this job had been everything and she'd blown it the minute she'd thrown Jake to the lions that were his parents.

The click of the car door opening startled her.

"Hey." Jake spoke softly, not wanting to scare her into driving away. He crouched down at the side of her. What he wanted more than anything was to hold her, tell her everything was going to be fine as he held her to his chest, but he knew if he moved too soon he'd ruin it. Instead, he let her adjust to him being beside her before he spoke again, watching as her breathing evened out and she appeared to calm to a degree. "How long have you been sitting here?" He knew she'd been there a while. He'd watched her for the last ten minutes before he'd dared to come outside.

"A few minutes, that's all. Don't worry, I haven't turned psycho stalker on you..."

"Baby, that's not what I meant. Are you okay?" His eyes gave her the once over. He had no idea where she'd been living for the last month. She looked tired, but not like she'd been sofa surfing for the last four weeks.

"Are you sober? If you're sober, I'm okay." Olivia risked a sideways glance at him. She wanted to see his eyes when he answered. Eyes could easily give away lies the body tried to conceal. She'd know instantly if he was lying, just from seeing those piercing steely blue eyes.

"I haven't touched a drop since you walked out. Seriously. Not one drop. It's all gone." He let that settle in, holding her gaze as she studied his face. He knew she was testing him, checking for any signs of a lie. He held solid, not faltering for a second. He'd learned his lesson the hard way. He'd lost her. But now she was there, sitting outside his house, and if there was any chance he could win her back he would grasp it with both hands. The house was an alcohol-free zone; every last drop had been removed. Izzie had refused to do it for him. She'd insisted he had to be the one to drain the bottles or it wouldn't make a difference. So he had. Every single hidden bottle was gone and he desperately wanted to prove himself to Olivia, if only she'd let him.

"Even the ones in my amp, you didn't know about those did you?" Jake stared at Olivia, he watched her intently as the stark realisation of the depths he'd sunk to, hit her. "Liv, I hid them all over the house, in the laundry room, the tumble dryer hose, I hid booze everywhere I knew you wouldn't think to look." He at least had the decency to look contrite. "But it's all gone. Every last drop. The house is a booze free zone."

He really had been a shit. Thinking hiding anything from her was an option in the first place had been his biggest mistake. If he was honest, he'd never had the strength to throw them all away until he'd lost her, but that had been his defining moment. The moment they talk about in all the rehab sessions. "I'm sorry. I really hurt you, didn't I? That was the last thing I wanted to do, but you have to know, that wasn't me. I would never hit you, not even when I'm wasted. I didn't mean to hit you that night at the beach house. I spun around and caught you, that's all. I would not hit you." He lowered his head as he gathered his thoughts again; the memory of that night chilled him. All he could see was her face when his hand had accidentally connected with her cheek. The sound haunted him, even now. "When I'm drinking I'm not the best version of me. It's the shittiest version of me. The one you should never have to see. The version I hope you never see again."

"You *hope?*" Olivia's face almost crumpled, her features hardening again as she weighed up his words. Her hands gripped the steering wheel so tightly that her knuckles were turning white.

Jake's eyes flicked from her tense hands back to her face. "Liv, I'm an alcoholic. I'll always be an alcoholic. I will always want a drink. Hopefully I'm strong enough to beat the cravings but I can't promise you I won't ever drink again. That's unrealistic and too much pressure for me." Jake lowered his gaze to the pavement below as he gathered his thoughts. He could feel her slipping away from him again. The next few minutes could ruin everything. "Forever is a long time. But today? Today, I'm sober." He looked her straight in the eyes, trying desperately to convey exactly how honest he was being with her. That was when it hit him. All the love he felt for her overwhelmed him. He'd do whatever it took to get her to stay.

"And yesterday? What about yesterday? Were you sober then?" Her fingers flexed around the leather of the steering wheel again.

"Yes. I've been sober for almost four weeks. I went to group therapy the day after you left, and yes, to answer the question you're not asking; I intend to be sober tomorrow, but I can't promise. I won't do that to you. I won't make promises I can't be sure I'll keep."

"Mmm." Olivia stared out of the windscreen, her eyes fixed forwards as she contemplated his words. Her shoulders relaxed as her head tipped forward slightly in an almost surrender-like gesture.

Jake seized his opportunity before it was lost for always. "Liv, can we go inside now?"

"I don't know if I can." She looked at him earnestly, tears welling in her eyes as she spoke. "I'm not sure, Jake. You hurt me. I can't do that again..."

"Baby, please, give me a chance. Give us a chance. You're here, that must mean something, right?" Jake hoped he'd judged his next move correctly. As he leaned into the car, he took the keys from the ignition then held out his hand to help her out of the car.

Olivia stared at his proffered hand. If she took it then she'd have to forgive him. If she didn't, well, she didn't know where that left her, apart from alone. And she wasn't good at being alone. She'd proved that time and again.

"Liv, just come in for five minutes. That's all I'm asking. Come and see for yourself I'm clean and sober. Please," he said, his hand held firm in front of her, almost begging her to take it. If she didn't he'd have to accept he'd blown everything and let her go. It would surely hurt him to watch her leave again, but if that was what she truly wanted, he'd let her leave.

Without speaking, she placed her hand in his, and swung her legs around and out of the car. As she stood beside him, he fought the urge to pull her into his body and just hold her there. Instead, he slammed the door closed behind her and clicked the lock on the key. He glanced down at their joined hands; it worried him how small hers appeared when encased in his. It was almost a symbol of her fragility and that scared him. Hurting her again scared him more than the thought that he may have a drink before the day was out.

"Thank you." It wasn't much but it was all he could offer in this moment.

"For what?"

"Trusting me enough to get out of the car." He tugged at her hand as he turned to walk towards the house. Olivia followed, tightening her grip on his hand as he guided them inside.

Arriving at the house for the second time that day seemed easier. Once inside, Jake refused to let go of her hand. He guided her toward the kitchen where he pushed the button on the coffee machine, sparking it to life. Still with her hand grasped firmly in his, he arranged cups and grabbed milk from the fridge. "Are you hungry? I can order takeaway."

"I haven't come back, Jake. I came to talk, that's all."

"Yeah I know, but we could eat if you're hungry. We can talk over dinner."

"Jake-"

"Don't, Liv. I know, okay." He glanced at their still

joined hands. His thumb rubbed along the back of her hand. "Just say you won't let go, just for now at least."

"Look, if you let go of my hand, I promise not to run. How does that sound?" The corner of her mouth turned up slightly at the uncertainty on his face. "I'll stay for a while. Even if you let go of my hand."

Jake chuckled. "That sounds good enough, and probably all that I deserve."

Reluctantly he let go of her hand, but only while he made the coffee. Once that was done, he resumed his place at the side of her, where his fingers laced casually with hers again. She sipped at her drink, and he waited for her to speak first.

"I'm sorry. For emailing your mum. That was stupid and none of my business, I was just trying to help you mend the rift but I know now that was wrong of me."

"It wasn't wrong of you to want to help me, I just wish you'd talked to me about it first. Could've saved us both a lot of heartache. My dad...well, let's just say it's their loss. I don't want to dwell on that shit anymore. I've learned that just because I'm their son it doesn't mean they have to like me. You grow up thinking that because they're your parents you deserve the unconditional love, perhaps that's how some families work, I don't know. Maybe one day... one day they'll realise I'm not the scum they think I am. They'll see that I just lost my way somewhere."

"So have you found it? Your way, I mean."

"I hope so. I don't know where this journey ends but I do know where it starts and if I take it one day at a time, I can do this. It gets easier each day." Releasing her hand again, he fumbled around in his pocket before pulling out a small coloured metal token which he proudly held aloft for her to see. "My one month token. I stopped going the first time before the month was up so I never got my token." His smile spread wide across his face. "See? I'm sticking with it this time. I will beat this." He allowed Olivia to take the small keepsake from him to look at. The next words to come out of his mouth were a risk but it was one he was willing to take. "But if you say you'll come home, it'll be so much easier. It'll give me even more reason to kick this for good."

"Don't do that. Don't put all that pressure on me, that's not fair." Handing the small disc back to him, Olivia took a step backwards. "You need to do this for you, nobody else."

"I am doing it for me. But I'm also doing it for you, for us. I want you back. I love you." There, the words were out there. He prayed she wanted the same things as he did.

Her heart almost stopped as the L word slipped from Jake's lips; it was all she'd wanted to hear him say for weeks. If only they could erase the last month, maybe everything would be okay then. Looking at him shyly with her smile almost apologetic, she spoke. "I love you too, but they're just words. Words are easy. Although I don't doubt how you feel, I have to protect myself from getting hurt again. I need to believe you want to beat this and that when you're well, you'll still want me."

Jake's hand reached up to tuck the strands of hair behind her ear, his fingertips caressing her cheek as his thumb trailed down towards her lips.

"Then come home and let me prove it."

CHAPTER
Thirty-Two

Walking into the shiny new building with its state of the art furniture and smell of fresh paint everywhere wasn't at all what Olivia had expected when Jake had asked her to come along. She'd been expecting a damp old community centre with the faint smell of urine hanging in the air; this was a polar opposite. Walking the short distance from the doorway to the reception desk, Olivia gave her name to the friendly-looking young receptionist that sat guarding the entrance. There wasn't a hair out of place. Her uniform looked more like that of airline staff than someone manning a drugs rehabilitation centre welcome desk.

After listening to the directions she'd been given, she headed off down the corridor, following a blue line that had been marked out on the floor. Why she couldn't come with Jake she had no idea, but he'd insisted that she meet him there instead. He'd been quite specific about that. So like the good girlfriend, she'd indulged him, and now there she was, one hour after he'd left the house.

As the blue line ended, there appeared to be some kind of waiting area where a few other people had gathered. Olivia spotted Izzie and Ben fussing over baby India, who was happily swaddled in her car seat. As she made her way over towards them, a side door opened and a man who appeared to be in his fifties, with thinning hair and a worn out jeans, greeted them.

"Good afternoon everyone. If you'd like to make your way inside, we're just about ready for you. There's tea and coffee if you'd like to help yourself before you take a seat." He waved his arm in a beckoning manner as he stood back, holding the door open so everyone could pass by him.

"Hey, I thought you weren't going to make it." Izzie wrapped an arm around Olivia, pulling her in for a hug. "Ben came with me so he can take India out if she kicks off, which is likely. The little angel doesn't do quiet on demand yet."

Olivia laughed as Ben fussed over his daughter, checking she wasn't too warm or about to throw up everywhere. "I don't think they're supposed to do anything on demand at four weeks old. You look amazing. Tired, but amazing."

"You don't need to suck up to me anymore, I don't employ you Jake does, but thanks. I feel like shit and I know I look like shit, but hey, today's about Jake, not me."

Leaving Ben to carry the baby in, the girls linked arms and walked through to where Jake sat waiting for them. He looked uncomfortable as he fidgeted with a thread on his sleeve. As soon as he saw them walking towards him, he stood to embrace Olivia. "You came."

"Of course I did. This is important to you, so where else would I be?" The lines around his eyes softened as he smiled. As Ben brought up the rear of the assembled crowd, Jake's attention turned to the baby. Bending down, he unwrapped the blankets swaddling her, unclipped the safety belt, and lifted her into his arms. India made a slight snuffling noise at being interrupted from her snooze, but soon settled into the crook of Jake's arm. "Hey there, beautiful." Jake stroked her tiny cheek. "Have you got a smile for Uncle Jake?" Right on cue, India's mouth curved into a precious grin, causing Jake to almost melt; this child had him wrapped around her finger. "That is not wind before you say it, Iz. That is a smile for her favourite uncle."

"Yeah, well don't let Alex hear you say that out loud." Izzie giggled.

"Hadn't we better sit down? Your guy is looking a bit antsy to say the least." Ben signalled towards the man who had opened the door a few moments ago.

As they sat down, Jake refused to hand India back. Instead, he sat cradling her in his arms, one of his big hands patting gently at her back. They sat in silence as Malcolm, the counsellor, ran through his much used, generic speech about hopes and dreams, the pitfalls of modern life, and lastly how far his current *family* group had come.

"I'm sure you're all anxious to get to the reason we're here today. Every single member in this room will today get their six month token. That means they haven't had a drink in 182 days. I think that deserves some recognition." Malcolm paused while everyone whooped and clapped. Baby India opened a beady eye, threatening to test out those brand new lungs, but when Uncle Jake whispered to her softly, she decided against it.

Olivia leaned in to whisper her own congratulations into his ear. He turned to capture her lips in a kiss before she had a chance to complain.

"Now, I'll invite each member of the family up here to accept their token." Malcolm switched his focus from the gathered supporting crowd to his so-called family group. "You are all welcome to say a few words if that's what you'd like to do, but it's not necessary. Your support network is here to simply celebrate how far you've come. Remember, inside this room, there is no pressure, no expectations, and no judging; merely support. So, with that in mind, can we have Rachel first, please?"

The room sat in silence as the group were called up to collect their sobriety token individually. Some of them said a few words of thanks to Malcolm, some spoke directly to their own invited people; some said nothing. Each person was applauded duly as they returned to their seat, only to be embraced by their loved ones.

"Now, we have Jake. Jake came to us six months ago after a short relapse in his journey, but I think he'd be okay with me telling you all that it's been a tough journey for him, But it's been one he's shown that he is more than ready to take now." Jake handed India back to her father before he left his chair to make his way to the front of the room. Shaking Malcolm's hand firmly, he took the small silver token offered to him and stood in front of the microphone in silence, just staring down at the disc as he spun it between his fingertips reverently.

After adjusting the microphone, he addressed the room. "Hey, I don't really know where to start. I started my twelve step journey a lot longer than six months ago, as Malcolm said, but I fell off the wagon. If I'm being honest, I don't think I was ever really on the wagon fully to begin with." He lowered his head, studying the small metal disc again, running the pad of his thumb over the number six on the front of it. "My girlfriend and boss will tell you that I used to hide my shit all over the place, thinking I was fooling them. The only person I was fooling was me." Jake took a quick drink from the water bottle he clutched in his fist, then held it up towards Olivia, smiling. "It's just water this time, baby."

"I know." Olivia kept eye contact with him, letting him know she trusted him.

"When I started this leg of my journey six months ago, I told myself I'd just stick with it until my girl came home. Sorry, Liv, but it's the truth, and if this group has taught me anything, it's taught me to be honest. So, here I am at six months without a drink. I can honestly say my way of thinking has changed. I don't want to drink anymore because I want to be a better man for my girlfriend." His eyes focused solely on Olivia, singling her out amongst the crowd. "Baby, you've helped me start my life again. I feel like this is the beginning. I have all the enthusiasm and energy back to do this. I'm so relieved you picked my side, that you have my back in all this madness. I couldn't imagine doing any of this without you, but what's more important is that I wouldn't want to. Thank you." His focus switched back to the whole room again. "I have to be careful not to get too full of myself, though, or let my guard down. As soon as you do that, the wave moves back in and takes over. I can imagine that, even years down the line, if you slip up, you'll be right back where you started. As of this moment, it's not that I don't want to drink again, I don't want to have to do the recovery again, and for me, that's enough to keep my on my road."

ACKNOWLEDGEMENTS

As always the biggest thank you goes to my other half, John. Without you I wouldn't be able to do this. You are my best friend and my world.

My children, Amy, Will and George - you make me proud every single day. Don't ever change, you're awesome.

Now for my fabulous editor, Karen – thank you, you are truly amazing at what you do and I want to shout it from the rooftops! I'm so honoured to have you not only as an editor but as a friend.

A big thank you to all the bloggers who work so hard to help the indie author community, you truly are an amazing bunch of people.

Lastly to all you readers, I couldn't do this without you. Love and hugs to every single one of you.

ABOUT THE AUTHOR

I live in the North of England with my husband and two of my three children, the eldest having flown the nest. Besides my motherly duties I run my own childcare business.

Finding time to write is hard to say the least, but it is something I absolutely love to do! You can usually find me sat with the laptop at odd hours of the day and night when the children are in bed. Dancing in the Rain, my first book, was self-published in February 2013. My second book, Taking A Risk, was released in July 2013.

My hope is that there will be many more books to follow, once I can drag myself away from all those social networking sites! Speaking of which you can find me on twitter, @carolinelou70, if you want to catch a glimpse of my insane ramblings!

Instagram

carolineeaston.wixsite.com/author

OTHER BOOKS

Risk Series

Taking A Risk

Worth The Risk

Risk It All

Blink

Dancing in the Rain

Printed in Great Britain
by Amazon